Elizabeth Crewe lives in Northumberland with her husband. She loves paintings, walks in the countryside and 'odd' antiques. She has worked as an actress in Repertory, both here and abroad, and for the National Theatre (on tour), as well as being on television and films.

She has worked in the past for the National Trust in East Anglia, helping with events, and was a co-founder of a Chamber Opera Company, helping to promote and give experience to up-and-coming young people.

Elizabeth Crewe

with best wishes

Elizabeth Crewe

THE ROAD

AUSTIN MACAULEY PUBLISHERS™

LONDON • CAMBRIDGE • NEW YORK • SHARJAH

A CIP catalogue record for this title is available from the British Library.

ISBN 9781528901086 (Paperback)
ISBN 9781528901093 (Hardback)
ISBN 9781528901109 (E-Book)

www.austinmacauley.com

First Published (2018)
Austin Macauley Publishers Ltd™
25 Canada Square
Canary Wharf
London
E14 5LQ

Acknowledgements

With thanks for their encouragement – R.C., F.M., S.D., L.A.

Chapter 1

Helen smiled to herself at the noise from the kitchen. It was the usual cacophony intermingled with murmuring voices, happy voices and laughter, for tonight was to be the last of the old and the beginning of the new for her beloved grand-daughter. Grandma, for that's who she was, sat back in the chair and gazed into the fire, 'I hope the future's good to Lucy and that Nick's a good man to her; they'll have their ups and downs just like anyone else, but I do hope she never...' Her mind went back to the past as she gazed at the fire; hers had certainly been an interesting life; whether the incidents that had happened to her over the years were justified or not, she wasn't sure; should she have changed her life when she was an arrogant over-privileged girl in her youth? Oh yes, most certainly, she should have listened more and considered her options knowing what she now knew, but then, everyone *would say that;* after all, wisdom only comes with age. Wisdom, had she learnt it or had it only been partially learnt, probably the latter for she'd always had a streak of 'now yesterday' and never 'perhaps tomorrow, when I've considered'. So many decisions she'd made had been so utterly stupid, she cringed with remembrance and willed the flames of the fire to burn and eradicate those decisions. Helen knew very well her short-comings and her lack of help to the family in 'educating' her grand-daughters; true, the money had been there but she'd always been too busy, too lost in her own little world and the work or man of the day, to think about anything else other than her own selfish whims; but somehow all was beginning to be well now and where one grand-daughter had viewed her with caution, there was now, after all the wilderness years, the glimmerings of hope for the future; but with the other one, Lucy, the Bride of Tomorrow, there and always had been an element of deep understanding.

At that moment, the door opened and her reverie was interrupted by Lucy, all red faced and glowing from the heat in the kitchen, bearing a tray of tea.

"Here we are, Granny," she said, "I'm afraid that dinner's going to be a bit late tonight as we're waiting for Mum's step-brother and step-sister to arrive with Dad at seven. Dad's said he'll meet them and be an extra pair of hands with the luggage, so you've got me for company for the next hour, I'm afraid."

"I can think of nothing nicer than to have you near me and a cup of tea as well, bliss! Do you know, I thought John and Meg were arriving tomorrow with their families; this really is good news, I'm so looking forward to seeing them all. Heavens, the house will be bursting at the seams, but at least your mother will have help before and after the wedding. Once you've gone, we'll all be sitting around talking about *their* weddings and speculating as to who's next!

"I think I'll miss that! What a pity Nick and I can't stay the night!"

"Don't be ridiculous, you'll be dying to get away and enjoy time with your new husband. Though I do remember your mother's father and I gate-crashing my parents' post wedding party and actually having a marvellous time."

"Grannie, you didn't really do that, did you?" Helen nodded and smiled impishly.

"Yes, we wanted to upset the apple cart; besides they were having lobster for dinner and champagne, and I could never resist lobster or champagne!"

Helen watched as Lucy poured out the tea and passed the cup to her. She was pleased to see that she'd used Helen's 'best' china, the 'Derby Posies' the tea set given to her as a wedding present all those years ago. It was still as bright as the day it had arrived, and she still loved it.

"Ah, my favourite tea set, thank you. I remember when it arrived all those years ago as a wedding present; your great-grandmother wouldn't put it out on display with the other gifts in case it was damaged. I tried to over-rule her but to no avail. It came from an old friend of hers, who had the most beautiful home, exquisitely furnished; as a child I was taken to the house for tea and told that I 'must really behave as Mrs Hannant was an interesting woman who'd been around the world several times!'."

And so began one of Helen's many reminiscences that were always such fun to listen to. Lucy settled down on the floor with her back up against her father's old chair and prepared to be entertained.

"Go on, Grannie, you can't stop now; we've both got our tea and there's time for you to reminisce. Anyway, I want to hear more about your past life, it seems rather colourful."

Helen paused, her mind going back through the aeons of time, then continued, "I think I was about eight and was quite over-awed as we drove up to the front door, it was a beautiful door, with an ornately carved fan-light above it and a lion's head knocker in heavy brass above the huge door knob and letter box; my mother rang the bell and then turned to check me, that is, checking that I was 'neat and tidy'. The door was opened by a wonderful old man who was Mrs Hannant's butler, very grey haired and with a stoop. He, like Mrs Hannant, became quite a friend to me and saved me from some awful scrapes, but that's another story. He ushered us into the hall, which was massive with marble pillars and a large staircase sweeping up from the hallway to the floor above. I remember the staircase was marble, too, with a central carpet and ornate metal embellishments running up the sides beneath the bannister, which was a dark wood, probably mahogany. In the middle of the hall was a round table with a large bowl of flowers; I suppose now, with my knowledge of flowers, they must have been lilacs.

"From beneath the stairs a door opened and an elegant and elderly lady came into the hall to greet us. I remember that she was much taller than my mother and had her hair piled up on top of her head and wore drop earrings. She was dressed in a lavender-coloured suit and cream blouse and had a set of lorgnettes dangling from a huge chain around her neck, these she lifted up to her eyes and peered down at me, offering me her hand which I took and shook carefully. She then greeted my mother and led us into the drawing-room, a beautiful room with windows from floor to ceiling opening onto a jewel of a garden, the scent of which filled the room. Tea came and went, having been served in this very tea set we're drinking out of. But it wasn't just the tea set that had left such an impression nor the garden, which I was allowed to go and explore, it was her *hands*, I'd never seen so many rings on so many fingers! I remember counting them, and on one finger alone there were three rings and on another; but what surprised me was that *every* finger, with the exception of her thumbs, had a ring on it, index, middle and little finger as well as the 'ring' fingers on both hands, and how they glittered, I was speechless! Soon it was time to leave and my mother and I duly said our 'farewells' and 'thanks' and left, but not before I'd shaken Mrs Hannant's hand again and watched the diamonds flash! My mother, your great-grandmother, kept looking at me all the way home and praising me for being so good. When my father came home the story had to be repeated, and finally I was asked 'why I'd been so quiet'. Finally, I told them both about Mrs Hannant's hands and the rings she wore and that 'I'd never seen anything like it before in my life, not even on the royal family'; my parents laughed and told me that ladies of her age who'd been left jewellery by deceased relatives usually wore everything, and it seemed in her case, the more the merrier, 'but in future I mustn't stare, that was rude'. Ever since then I've always loved jewellery, but I've never worn that amount! Now though, any elderly person I've met I've automatically been drawn to their hands but have never again seen such a display."

Lucy and her grandma laughed, and Lucy poured out another cup of tea.

"What a story, I'm amazed you can remember it so well."

"As you get older, things from the past have a habit of seeping into your mind like wonderful pictures, everything so vivid, almost hearing voices and the conversations that occurred. Strange, isn't it? Some of the bad things come back too but not often."

"So how did this tea set come into the family?"

"Oh, that happened many years later. I had a party for my eighteenth birthday at home and my parents gave a cocktail party as well and, of course, Mrs Hannant came too, driven down by her butler, old Mr Curtis. He waited in the car as Mrs Hannant never stayed long at a party, only about an hour; she used to tell me that the 'best time to leave was when everyone wanted you to stay'. I've abided by that rule ever since, it's saved me from an awful lot of bores! Anyway, at that party she told me that when I got married, my wedding present from her was going to be the 'Derby Posies' as I'd always admired it, and that's how it's come to be in the family."

Lucy looked at her cup and examined it carefully; her grandmother smiled to herself. Lucy spoke,

"I hope it's never damaged now I know the story. You know, it's a bit of history isn't it, and somehow 'belongs' to us all; I'm so glad it's in the family."

She smiled wistfully to herself, the old lady looked at her grand-daughter fondly, 'Yes,' she mused, 'you're like me, in a world of 'fond imaginings', but she's learning, the past *is* the beginning of the future. Perhaps I should let the tea set go to her now and not later.' She decided she'd think about it, not rush things.

"Are there anymore tales, Grannie, of your past?"

"Oh plenty, some I'm not quite sure about, others I'd prefer to forget, too stupid for words!"

"Please tell me, I've read a lot about the 'fifties' and I've liked what you've told me, like going to the 'Festival of Britain' and the 'Ideal Home Exhibition' at Olympia and making your own kind of fun. It's old-fashioned, I know, but it seems to have been such a time of hope."

"Yes, there was 'hope', and espresso coffee bars, and starching our petticoats with sugar and water, and not being able to sit down because they'd melt with the heat of your body and stick to you in awkward places."

"That's right." They both laughed, Lucy looking at her wide-eyed, "Heaven's how awful, what on earth did you do?" the girl said.

"Nothing really, just hoped it was soon time to go home, as by then our 'winkle-picker' toed shoes, as they were called, were killing us! I suppose it depended how fond you were of the current boyfriend as to whether you took them off or not; you see, most people had to walk home from a 'gig' as you call it, there was rarely a lift and certainly no buses after midnight. I was one of the lucky ones who was always picked up by one father or another, so never had to worry about being 'man-handled', as we called it, on the way home."

"Does that mean you were a virgin when you married?"

"Most certainly, it was still considered very bad form if you were 'damaged goods' and believe me, word soon got around if you were 'easy meat', so we never 'indulged', so to speak. We all knew what happened, but it rarely crossed our minds to 'try it out', besides it was considered 'something special', a bonding to happen on our wedding night. I know things are different now and in some ways perhaps it's a good thing; after all, if I'd indulged I'd never have married your mother's father, a homosexual, and suffered the trauma of being married to a man who was 'doing things' almost by the book because he had to; but that's a part of my life I never talk about."

She looked at Lucy sternly, the girl knew not to question; on a lighter note she said,

"Well then, tell me another of your early memories, they're fun to hear and we've got time."

Helen looked at the girl, wishing she could be left in peace for a while but realising that tonight of all nights, this was never going to happen!

"Well, there is one story, whether *you'll* find it funny is entirely up to you, because in this day and age it's *positively old-fashioned* and that's why I cringe every time I think about it, but it's true and really did happen to me, I was 'caught in the act'."

"Sounds intriguing," said Lucy, "so go on, what are you waiting for?"

"Funnily enough, me, I'm trying to sort out in my mind the relevant facts and leave out the dross, but I don't think I can. Do you really want to sit patiently and listen to the ramblings of your old grandmother, wouldn't you rather be in the kitchen doing something?"

"No, you forget I'm the bride, focus for tomorrow, and anyway, you're more fun to be around!" Lucy replied with alacrity.

Her grandmother looked askance at her and realised that today there'd be no little 'rest' in front of the fire, so she might as well carry on; after tomorrow life would seem rather dull once Lucy and Nick had gone.

"All right, my dear, here goes. When I was a student I was living at home. Life and work went on, exams taken and passed, luckily, and boyfriends came and went. I remember that one was an eccentric biochemist and used to write to me as *Dearest Half-*

wit, which upset my parents but pleased the postman, who took great delight in shouting *'It's for dearest half-wit again, another card from Ireland!'* Our meeting of minds was the theatre and books. Beyond that nothing! At the same time my great friend Karen, who lived over the road from me, had a brother who was utterly gorgeous and was training to be a vet. I longed to be 'his' but to no avail, I had glasses and his girlfriend had long legs, a complete 'no-brainer', as you say. One summer a group of us opted to go to Barcelona University on a summer Spanish language course; we all knew we'd learn very little but it would be fun.

"On the way back to the airport, David, trainee vet and Karen's brother, announced that we girls had to do something for him. Whilst we'd all been working he'd been gathering items for research and wanted to take them back to England…illegally. So, two geckos, some beetles in a box, various items which I don't remember, plus two eggs came home. The geckos bit his girlfriend, so end of the romance; the beetles disappeared; and I managed to get the eggs back inside my bra, without breakage, these hatching three days later as geckos! We all agreed to meet up again in a fortnight for a car rally and party and the time passed very quickly. In those days, except for engagement parties and twenty-firsts, all parties were held in people's houses with friends' fathers acting as 'bouncers'; there were always gate-crashers who'd heard about the party in the coffee bars, and they were ceremoniously picked up by their pants and thrown out of the front door by whichever fathers were acting as security. We soon got used to this and usually cheered, something that no one would dare do now, very un-PC!

"The rally was great fun and I was paired up with a boy called Michael, who was driving his father's V8 Pilot, a most luxurious car at the time. We got on well and had soon guessed the clues and picked up the various 'finds' that had been deposited on the route. Michael and I won the rally and were duly presented with our prizes, he a book and me chocolates, I so wanted it the other way around but said nothing. The table groaned with food and the drink flowed; in those days it was usually beer for the boys and either soft drinks or Babycham for the girls!"

"What on earth was 'Babycham'?"

"I really don't know, but I do know I drank it and felt very sophisticated; it was usually served with a cherry in it and tasted like odd fizzy lemonade but did have some alcohol in it. It was, I suppose, the poor man's champagne."

"Yuk, how horrid," replied Lucy. "I'm glad I've never tasted that, but I do love the 'bubbles' we have now! Please go on, I'm sorry I interrupted you."

"Well, the evening wore on and someone had brought records, Bill Haley and the Comets and Frank Sinatra among some, I remember, there would have been more. Time moved on and I suddenly realised I was late getting home. As I only lived on the other side of the road, I wasn't too bothered until I realised I had no key to get into the house. David, Karen and Michael escorted me home, the boys deciding to 'knock' my father up and explain what had happened, but Karen said 'why disturb him when there's bound to be a ladder in the garage that'll reach Helen's window and she can climb in.' Good idea, no one would be disturbed, brilliant! We all crept around the back and sure enough, the garage door was unlocked and the hoses that had been watering the garden still *in situ*, and leaning up against the wall was a ladder which was duly removed and leant against the wall under my window. It was decided that David would climb up into my bedroom and whilst Michael held the ladder at the bottom, I'd climb up too and then David would come back down. All went well until I climbed the ladder and tried to get in over the window sill and my dress caught on the thorns of the roses outside my window and I was left dangling half out and half in my bedroom. To cap it all, there was a bird nesting in the rose and it started flapping about under my skirt. David told me to hurry up as someone would wake up and see him, and I explained that I was caught on the bush and that a bird was flapping about under my skirt. 'Never mind that, just free yourself and let me get down again' came the agitated cry; with super human effort I freed myself, but as I pulled myself in, a voice from the next bedroom window boomed out.

'What on earth are you doing in my daughter's bedroom?'

'I'm not in, I'm getting out, sir.'

'Even so, what on earth possessed you to get in in the first place?' enquired my father.

Lucy sniggered at this.

"You're right to snigger, so did the others at the foot of the ladder; my father told David to get me in and I was unceremoniously hauled into my bedroom. I then lent out and told my father about forgetting the key and deciding not to wake anyone by climbing in through the window. By this time David was halfway down the ladder when my father told him to come back in and not dirty his trousers and he'd let him out through the front door; this David did with myself and the other two watching in amazement as he disappeared out of my bedroom and down the stairs, he forgot about the cat halfway up the stairs and hissed an apologetic 'sorry' as he continued down to the hall, he also forgot about the very crude burglar alarm that went off and not only woke our house but everyone else in the neighbourhood. Needless to say, he was let out and I was given a dressing down the next day, now you know why I've never forgotten the incident."

Lucy laughed, "I can see why, even so I enjoyed hearing about it."

"To this day, I honestly believe that all the scrapes I got into, and had to be rescued from, were because of being too vain and refusing to wear my glasses. It's a funny thing but when you can't see, your hearing seems impaired and certain things become distorted and this gets worse the older you get." She looked at Lucy, whose face was a blank. "Oh well, perhaps it's me, I've never been good at concentrating, my brains have always been several steps ahead of my 'seeing' so I've missed things, and now I'm too old to be bothered."

"No Grannie, you're a barrel of laughs, but I still love you and always will. I suppose I'd better go back to the kitchen and leave you to rest."

With that the girl got reluctantly to her feet and went over to her grandmother, gave her a kiss and picked up the tray. Her grandmother felt relief at being alone for a while and then remembered something important she wanted to give to the girl.

"Don't go just yet, put the tray down, I've something to give you, and you may like to wear it tomorrow or sometime on your honeymoon. When I was young my father gave me a present when he came home from Pakistan for his mother's funeral; I think you should have it now." She pulled an old box out of her pocket and gave it to the girl, she continued, "I've been carrying this around with me for days, deciding whether or not to give it to you, but I think the time is right." Lucy took the box and opened it, inside was a sapphire and diamond cross-over ring with diamond shoulders, she gasped. "I've always loved this ring and wanted it to go to someone extra special. I believe you'll look after it well and wear it often."

Lucy hugged her grandmother, "I'll always love it and think of you every time I wear it. I know it'll bring me luck, look it fits." She gazed at it, her grandmother watching her, knowing she'd done the right thing.

"Now, my dear, take it away with you and please will you leave me to have a little snooze? Tonight's going to be hectic and none of us will be in bed before midnight, too many excited voices. Besides, in a little while, I must wake your 'Grumps' as you call him; he'll be so pleased to see everyone and he's so excited about tomorrow, how good of you to ask him to read the lesson, he'll do it so well."

Lucy picked up the tray and after a last look at the old lady, who was settling back into the chair, her mind on other things and her eyes drooping against the warmth of the firelight, left the room. Helen smiled to herself, her mind drifting back over all they'd talked about and all that had happened during her life and soon she slept…and dreamed…

Chapter 2

Helen found herself dreaming a lot during her rest, possibly because she'd been talking with Lucy about the past. It was amazing what came creeping back into her subconscious, things she had no wish to remember and yet there they were in brilliant 'technicolour'.

Marriage, her first, was to a business man, a man far and away different from the life she'd been brought up to and the professional young men she'd known. In fact, she went out with him as a direct rebellion against the cloying attitude of her elitist life. She'd had various boyfriends from the Army and Navy and suddenly wanted to be free to choose for herself, not be 'attached' to someone who was of the 'right background'. Too late, she realised her mistake. She'd married a physically brutal man, but one who could also be caring, a psycho; his *bonhomie*, generosity and humour to all who came near had impressed her and her innocence had been such that she'd taken it all in. She thought before her marriage that here was a man who'd not only work hard and care for her but be totally different from any in her past life. She liked the idea of being married to a businessman and felt, with his guidance, she'd be an asset to him. So the marriage went ahead; it was lovely, so many friends, so much fun. Afterwards, she embraced everything that happened each day that dawned and tried hard to understand his business, and at first all went well, they were happy and got on well, she learnt fast. Then came the lies, the deceit, never the plaudits always the blame; 'where was the money?' 'We thought your family was wealthy, where's your clothes' allowance and money for a house?' And then he'd hit her or trip her up and laugh when she fell. His mind changed and he became schizoid, life with him became dangerous, but what to do...? She could do nothing, she could not leave; after all where would she go, and with a child.

One day, six weeks after Charlotte was born, his sister came around to talk to him. Helen remembered watching a programme and suddenly being asked to leave, she refused as the programme was nearly over. This provoked a rage. She looked at him petrified, her sister-in-law too; it was then that he hit her and savagely dragged her by her hair into the kitchen and kicked her in the stomach and stamped on her legs. From then on she never knew how she'd be at the end of the day and lived in constant fear, and so the years progressed. Her parents had wanted her to break her engagement as they could see what he was and the vicious temper he had; but no, she'd made a promise, therefore she must keep it, so their final words to her were 'you've made your bed, now lie on it'. And so she did, never mentioning any of the hurt she felt on an almost daily basis, carrying on in a deeply spiralling ring of unhappiness, knowing she had to go on for the sake of her daughters.

She started to find happiness again, watching the growth and development of the two girls, two such different characters; the elder studious and quiet, a lover of family, particularly the older members; the younger full of 'bounce' and 'joie de vivre', eager to find out about life, a gregarious child forever sunny. They filled Helen's life with such fulfilment that her husband's odd behaviour failed to awaken suspicion as to his developing orientation. He'd always been interested in the arts, never in sport, and he'd always had a penchant for elderly ladies, never their friend's wives. Helen had accepted this as part of his so-called 'charm' and actually felt a feeling of warmth whenever they complemented her on having such a good husband. 'You're such a lucky girl,' they'd say, 'make sure you look after him, he'll never stray. He's such a good father to those dear little girls!' She'd smile and say "thank you" and wonder what would face her when they returned home. Always there was the incessant questioning as to whom they'd met and what had been said, always the asking again and the raised fist if she said something different to what she'd said earlier. In the end she took a notebook with her wherever she went and wrote everything down and gave it to him when she was home, but even then she'd be questioned; and so life went on, sometimes sunny other times cruel, until one day… He came into the kitchen where she was preparing the evening meal and the children's food, as usual he started trying to put things away, irritated at how untidy the place was; as usual she said nothing but just took things out again and carried on preparing, dreading what might come next.

"I'm seeing the doctor today, I've an appointment at two pm. I'm going about the pain in my stomach and other things."

"Other things, are you feeling really ill?" asked Helen carefully, "I know you've been away on business a lot, do you think you've picked up a bug?"

"Probably, but I won't know until I've been, will I? I'll tell you what's to be done later at dinner, by the way what mess are you preparing?"

"Fish, why?"

"No reason, just wondering if I'll be able to eat it now your cooking's ruined my gut."

With that he'd picked up the keys to the car and disappeared. It was a sunny day and Helen decided to go out in the garden with the girls and do some planting with them in their new vegetable patch. They'd moved recently to a pair of converted cottages, and the feuding seemed to have stopped and an uneasy truce settled in. She thought about her husband and whether he really was ill, certainly he'd been spending more and more time away from home, blaming the slump in business and meetings in Birmingham as the cause, and in fact, business everywhere was down so she'd never worried, but now…her mind started to question…could there be another woman…? She couldn't imagine there was as he'd never been remotely interested in sex after the girls were born, and she'd always remembered her late mother-in-law's comments on sex, 'how it always faded once children arrived but then companionship set in'. Helen's naivety had accepted this, she had no mother to ask whether this was normal behaviour, her parents were away in the Far East on a tour of duty, so she had no knowledge how the intimacy of married life should develop, so she accepted what her mother-in-law said as normal.

"Mummy, look, a really wriggly worm!" Her reverie was interrupted by her daughter climbing all over her and depositing a very large worm in her lap. Helen hated worms, slugs and snails, even though the youngest daughter and her sister would have snail races on the kitchen floor and invite their friends for tea with the admonition to 'bring their own snails'. The kitchen floor would be covered in slime from the wretched things, and she'd spend hours washing the floor afterwards, but always a forgotten snail would creep out from under the kitchen cupboards nonchalantly, willing her to stand on it. She felt sure they did it deliberately, the eyes always seemed to leer at her!

"Gosh, he is a big one, isn't he? Don't you think he'd prefer to be in your veggie patch, helping to aerate the soil?"

"Oh yes, but I thought you'd like to see him first. He's got lots of segments and so many colours and if you put him on paper, you can hear him move. Pick him up, Mummy, he won't bite." The worm was picked up and solemnly put into her mother's hand; she tried to look happy but felt sick.

"Take him away now, please, as he mustn't get too hot. Go and find a very cool spot for him and bury him before a blackbird picks him up." The worm was grabbed in a little fist and she watched as her daughter went back to her sister. Just then, her husband appeared around the corner of the house, looking very pale and agitated; she stood up and looked at him.

"What is it, what's he said? Shall I make some tea?"

"No thanks, are the girls all right on their own? The doctor has told me I must speak to you, and I'd rather be alone with you when I do."

"Yes, they're planting, and Charlotte won't stop until she's finished and Sophie's too engrossed in picking up worms not to stay with her. Let's go into the conservatory. We can keep an eye on them both from there."

He followed her into the room and started pacing up and down; she knew from past experience not to speak. Finally, after quite a time of pacing he sat in the chair opposite to her and spoke.

"I've fallen in love," he blurted out, 'So it's true,' she thought, there *is* another woman, then the bombshell, "with a man."

She tried to speak but couldn't, her mind was racing but words wouldn't come. She looked at the anguished man facing her, searching for *what* from her…approbation, revulsion, disbelief at what had been said, she just didn't know what to say or feel…that was it…not words, but *her feelings* that were hurting, she'd been betrayed. She was hurt, then angry, that after all these years of trauma, there'd been no need for her suffering and endless brutal abuse; he could have told her what was wrong years ago and given her a divorce. Instead, he'd lived a lie and made both their lives miserable, but could he have done otherwise? Homosexuality was still a taboo subject, only just de-criminalised. She wondered, had he had to fight his feelings all these years too? Poor man, what a burden to carry around day after day, what a lie it must have been all these years to have *pretended to be normal* and known he was *failing*. No wonder he'd never made love to her all these years, but lain there sometimes trying but invariably turning onto his back, his fists clenched, not knowing what to do, never once stopping to touch her belly when she was pregnant but rather recoiling with revulsion at her changing figure; she remembered now, the fear etched on his face as he regarded her then; now she was beginning to understand WHY his anger had been so apparent. She looked at him and spoke with complete calm,

"What does he suggest you do? Actually no, what would *you* like to do? Whatever you decide I'll support you; all I ask is that we try and keep things as calm as possible in front of the girls and continue as normal until you've really thought about things carefully and where you want to be."

"Yes, I promise I'll do that, I owe you that," his face brightened malevolently, "on one condition, *you allow him to come and stay, and meet him.*"

She felt herself and her spine tingle with disgust that he could suddenly change his mood and be so cavalier with her and her needs. How dare he behave like a 'love-struck' teenager as though it were an everyday occurrence and part of life's pattern and plan. This 'man' had ruined her marriage in the same way as another woman, flung into the bin twelve years of a family life that, for all his now known faults, had grown and prospered, but what now? In that moment any thought of care and respect for him disappeared for ever, now she knew that it must be 'each day as it came' and her quelled anger had to be repressed, common sense and dignity must prevail.

"I'll do that, but not yet, you must give me time to try and understand, and also, decide what *I* want to do; it's not just me it's the *girls* too."

He stood up and looked out at the garden and the two little girls, who were happily playing, he then turned to his wife and looked into the cold eyes of betrayed trust and said,

"I need a drink and you'll need one too."

He disappeared into the kitchen and soon returned with a glass of wine for Helen and a martini for himself, he gave Helen hers, trying to lock eyes with her and 'see' what she was thinking. Nothing, was the answer there, Helen was numb, drained, she suddenly felt dirty but knew she could not relax until after the girls had gone to bed. It was she who'd written the rules for so-called 'normality' and it was 'she' that would make sure everything was. She decided that her parents had to be told and her closest friend but no one else. She knew that her father would be stunned but not surprised; she'd leave it up to him to tell her mother. Her mother, her aunts and their mother, her grandmother whom he doted on, would think she'd 'made it up' and they'd ridicule her, tell her she was 'dreaming' and to stop having 'thespian thoughts', but her father would understand, but how would he react?

"Thank you," she said looking up; she drank the wine almost in one and asked for another, he brought it, this time she said nothing just drank. "I'll give the girls their tea and put them to bed, that'll give you time to think and try and decide how we are all going to live, will you want him here? Will you be here or there with him? Let's talk in a little while after dinner."

She called to the girls and two dirty and happy little bodies came running into the conservatory.

"Tea's ready, let's wash your hands, give Daddy a kiss." She disappeared into the kitchen, not wanting to see the girls in their father's arms, knowing that after tonight she'd have to play 'happy families', but then, the initial shock would be over so it might not be so bad. She decided to be stoic and take all the comments and probable insults in her stride, it was the girls' future happiness that must never be taken into doubt. Suddenly there was a little face at her knee,

"I've put the worms away, Mummy, will they mind the dark?"

"No darling, because that's where they belong."

Her other daughter was at her side now, and she cuddled her tightly, she wriggled,

"Ow, that hurts, Mummy. Do you know, Sophie dug up all the plants again just to put her worms in the holes, so I've had to plant them all again, tell her not to touch them as my lettuces will never grow, nor will the radishes."

A little muddy face looked up at her mother.

"Oh dear, Sophie, you're in bother now, but Charlotte's right, we must now leave everything to grow and just water them every night when it doesn't rain, and do you know, the worms will love helping too." The child grinned up at her, showing a row of muddy teeth. "You've not been eating earth again, have you?"

"And she tried to eat a worm but I stopped her," said Charlotte; her sister grinned harder and pulled at her frock.

"What am I going to do with you both?" The girls giggled and hugged their mother.

She gave them both a kiss and they ran off to wash their hands; she knew there'd be a mess but somehow that was never going to matter again, an awful burden was lifting; still a long way to go but a glimmer of warm light was on the horizon, and with understanding life would get better eventually. In a little while the girls were fed and taken up to bed for a bath and story; she deliberately put too much bubble bath in the water so that they'd be everywhere, the girls squealed with delight and soon a 'batting game' with the bubbles was well under way and they all became soaked. Helen failed to notice the discarded pants and socks and the KY jelly until her husband came into the bathroom and tried surreptitiously to put the clothes in the linen basket and the tube of jelly in the cupboard; she made to speak to him, but turned back to the girls and washed their backs.

"I thought I'd read to the girls tonight, do you mind?" he ventured.

"No, go ahead, I've rather a lot of clearing up to do here."

She lifted the girls out of the bath and started drying their protesting little bodies, soon they'd disappeared, each clutching a favourite toy into their beds, thumbs in mouths, waiting to be read to. She listened as her 'husband', that was of two hours ago, started reading 'Winnie the Pooh' in his clear voice, all was quiet, the girls were listening. She cleared up the bathroom and then opened the cupboard door and took out the tube he'd put there and examined it, she found she couldn't continue after reading what it was made of and what it was for, her imagination was working overtime, she'd ask him later. She returned it to the cupboard and went into the girls' room; he'd nearly finished, Sophie's eyes were drooping and Charlotte was struggling to concentrate, then the book was closed and half-hearted protests were uttered by two sleepy and sweet-smelling children.

"That's it, no more tonight, you're both dropping to sleep. Goodnight, you two." He bent down and kissed them and left the room; she was glad now it was her turn to tuck them up, kiss them and smell the perfume of their freshly washed bodies, one of her favourite 'chores'.

"Night, night, Mummy, hope the worms are all right and not cold, I'll find them a toy tomorrow," snuffled Sophie and promptly slept.

"Love you, Mummy," two arms enfolded themselves around their mother's neck. "Tomorrow I'll put in some onions, will you help me, please?"

Helen looked down at Charlotte and hugged her and ruffled her hair,

"'Course I will, darling, but now you must sleep, night, night."

She checked the window and the curtains and kissed the two girls again and left them. Out on the landing she suddenly paused and looked in the direction of *their* bedroom, a thought came to mind, 'Who sleeps where from now on? I can't share a bed with him, and he certainly won't ever want to be near me again, let's hope something's resolved tonight when we talk.' She went back to the kitchen and started cooking the fish, he came in from the garden and her thoughts were answered.

"You can go in the spare room from now on, I'll keep the main bedroom. Oh, and I've just spoken to John, he's coming for the weekend. I'm picking him up at four tomorrow and then we'll go back to Birmingham on Monday morning or Sunday night, so we'll need to eat at night and lunch on Sunday. I'll take him out on Saturday. Oh, and by the way, I've decided to divorce you, so find a lawyer, you're not much to live with anymore."

He turned on his heel and took his drink out into the garden, she watched his back. 'So that's how it's to be is it, all decided and certainly no talking tonight. I can only hope that this John has more manners and will explain, but I'll not go into the spare room, he and his paramour can do that.' After a quick smile she muttered to herself, "I'll make it special for them."

She called after him, "I think I'll stay in the main bedroom, after all there are more of my things in there and they'll take too long to move in such a short space of time. After your bombshell, it's now time for me to call the shots, and I'm staying put, after all it's the place the girls know when they need a hug or are sick." She waited for the anger to erupt but none came, she continued, "I'm sure the spare bedroom can be made special for you both and it's got its own bathroom." How strange before she'd even met this man she was being practical and acknowledging him. The reply came from the garden,

"OK. you're right, but don't think it's going to be this easy for you, I still want a divorce and I'll dictate terms. Remember you own nothing, everything you've got has come from me. Your family's paid for nothing."

They ate their dinner in an uneasy silence, punctuated by the odd banal remark, she asking about 'John's' preferences with food, was he a vegan, vegetarian or a normal eater, what did he like to do, where did he like to go, did he like the theatre, music books anything, just to get the present evening over with. In the end she found herself quite looking forward to the next day and meeting 'John'. The evening was warm and they both sat in the conservatory, he smoking she just reading. Occasionally she'd catch him looking at her, so she smiled and asked if there was anything he needed, a shake of the head being his reply; she tried to talk but couldn't, she wanted to but where to start? She didn't want to be argumentative nor tearful, that was for others who wore their hearts on their sleeves, nor vengeful that got you nowhere, besides she'd had enough of 'rage' all through the long and watchful years of her marriage that had now disintegrated. No, they were adults, and she felt that after this weekend had passed, they'd be able to talk and good sense would prevail. Finally, she closed her book and told him she was going to bed but she'd put fresh towels and his 'PJs' in the spare bedroom.

"Goodnight, I hope you sleep well," a grunt came from the other side of the room and she'd gone, escaped to hopeful oblivion and peace of sorts. She wondered if he'd sleep but didn't much care.

The following day 'John' appeared, carrying a large bunch of her favourite roses, he shook her hand and pecked her on the cheek; her 'husband' hovered in the doorway nervously watching. She'd decided she'd only ever refer to him from now on by his name, never the shortened version nor an endearment.

"Something smells good, oh, and a pie, I love them, is the fruit from around here? William said you make good pastry."

Helen was stunned at his easy manner and involuntarily smiled at him, "Thank you for the flowers, they're lovely and my favourites too."

"John's hobby is as a florist, as well as being in business, it helps him relax."

"Really, how nice." She watched as he took the vase from her and deftly started arranging the flowers for her. His fingers were long and beautifully manicured; she studied his face, strange it wasn't unlike William's, a good profile, hair a deep Titian colour and eyes a deep brown. He was lean and tanned.

"Where would you like these?" he said, turning and smiling at her. William indicated the drawing-room and they both disappeared.

She heard William take John upstairs to the bedroom, both chattering away and the odd comment from John about the furniture or paintings he saw. She was busy concentrating on the sauce and failed to notice the black robed figure beside her; she'd felt *'it'* several times in the last few weeks since they'd moved to the house, but now she saw *'it'* clearly beside her, no face nor hands but she knew it was *'real'*. The spectre stood beside her before turning and vanishing; the last time had been when William was mowing the lawn, and it'd hovered behind him. To Helen 'it' was like the cloaked and hatted man on the Sandeman's port label. Was this a portent of what was to come, was it a warning? She decided to be wary in all things. She'd heard a story about a ghost that appeared sometimes from people in the village, whenever 'a sadness was about to happen'. It was the ghost of an old priest who, during the plague years in the seventeenth century, would walk across the fields and hills visiting his parishioners until one day he fell into a bog and drowned. He'd been quite a hero, some said, and sheltered Cavaliers from the Roundheads during the Civil War; he'd been 'much loved', many had seen him but no one had been 'harmed'.

Just then the two men returned, flushed, into the kitchen, her 'husband' noticeably more so. 'He's not used to this,' she thought, 'there's a very rude awakening coming soon.'

"Let's all have a drink," said John, "I've brought some beautiful wine I picked up in France on my holiday, as a present for you both, I do hope you'll like it."

So the weekend progressed and was over, and Helen found herself looking forward to his frequent visits, and even the girls took no notice of the odd arrangements now in place and accepted John as a really fun man to have around who took them out riding and for walks and told them about nature. They brought back all manner of insects and animals to look after, he even taught them how to make a 'hide' for the adders and newts and hedgehog houses for the winter and bird houses for the spring. Finally, he was a fantastic cook, and made sweets! During the weeks of that summer Helen had told her parents what had happened. The row that ensued afterwards was exactly as she'd imagined it would be, her father incensed at the hurt done to her and the attack on her femininity, her mother in tears and the rest of the family in utter disbelief. She'd had to protect the girls from her parents as no one could foresee the odd outburst of 'fondness' for John that inevitably came forth when they told stories of what he'd done with them. Her father was enraged that she'd allowed the girls to go and stay with John and their father and felt it was 'crass stupidity' on her part, did she really want to exist in such a *ménage à trois*? Arguments had developed with the aunts and her grandmother, with her father accusing them all of being 'disloyal' to her, to such an extent she'd brought the girls home, and remained, refusing all invitations to the contrary. However, she could not escape the vitriolic phone-calls which William usually answered; she'd retreat down the garden with the girls to the 'veggie patch' and weed. She found after a time that she liked John, he made her laugh and together they'd talk about all the things she loved, until jealousy from her 'husband' set in. One day it got too much and the bubble burst, William had been particularly provoking and an argument had ensued, a 'voice' in Helen's head said, *'This threesome cannot go on, it must be stopped'* The shouting started and she listened as the expletives were hurled this way and that, finally William said to John,

"I don't need you or her, but don't worry, I'll still see you, you're a good fuck."

Helen left the silence of the room quietly, the eyes of the two men bloody daggers in her back; she left them to their shouting, which soon resumed and paused on the stairs, the pain and humiliation of the early years of her marriage came flooding back, the pretence and ugliness nauseatingly real. She closed the bedroom door and went to bed.

The following morning, as usual, the girls came into her bed with a book to be read to them; they snuggled down beside her and she started on the story. She loved this quiet time they had together at the weekend, her Teasmade going off for tea, the girls with their milk and biscuits, the cat on the bed as usual and the dogs at the end of it, half an hour of happiness and peace. Soon it was time to get up, they'd all decided what they wanted for breakfast and were on their way down, Sophie running ahead with the dogs Charlotte lagging behind. Suddenly, Helen stopped and listened at the unknown moans and realised they were the sounds of illegal passion coming from the spare room, she froze as a little hand was slipped trustingly into hers, and then, a heart-rending moan of supreme passion or pain filtered through the door and the voice of Charlotte at her side asked,

"Is Daddy being hurt?"

Tears came into her eyes and she looked down at her daughter, into the child's questioning eyes, those windows into her vulnerable brain that was trying to comprehend the unnatural sound. The vulgarity of the adult world had seeped its wormwood and gall into childhood.

"No darling, all's well, let's go and feed the dogs."

The child smiled, in the moment of her mother's reassurance the noise forgotten, and ran down the stairs to her sister and the animals. Helen stared at the door, 'This is the end; tomorrow, when you're both gone, I'll seek help. How I hate you both now, for your indecent behaviour within the hearing of an innocent, our daughter; and me, what am I now, you've deflowered my femininity and reduced me to filth.' She walked purposefully down the stairs and to a new life, whatever that might be.

Chapter 3

The following day William and his 'friend' left without a word, not to Helen nor to the girls, the car disappearing in a cloud of dust down the track.

"Now it begins, mine and the girls' new life. But first, to get rid of the dross and eleven years of abuse. I'm thirty-four, there's plenty of life ahead and my girls will never suffer, if I can help it. How dare that bastard think he can ride roughshod over us and get away with it! And as for your 'friend', William, you're welcome to him, he may have broken up our marriage but neither of you has fazed me or broken my spirit; whatever you both do I'll still come out on top."

Helen went back inside and found the girls playing with the dogs and getting their bowls ready for their evening meal. Charlotte and Sophie came over to her,

"Have they gone, Mummy?"

"Yes, they've gone."

"Good," said Charlotte, "I never liked my father, much less his friend, so good riddance to bad rubbish."

She spooned the dog's food into the bowls with renewed vigour. Sophie looked at her sister wide-eyed and carefully put the first of the bowls on the floor.

"Do you really not like Daddy, Charlotte, should I not like him too?"

"You can do what you like, but I hate him."

With that Charlotte went out of the room, closely followed by her confused sister; what Charlotte would say to her sister Helen hadn't a clue, but she'd sort it out when the problem arose. Helen finished putting the bowls on the floor and then started thinking about what to do whilst preparing the girls' tea. She decided to consult a lawyer well away from where they lived and then thought again, money would now be tight and cuts would have to be made, she'd have to think again. In the end she drew up a list of the pros and cons of the whole divorce, scenario including the evidence she'd have to produce, and once she'd thought of that her mind went back to the events of the morning and she felt dirty and washed and re-washed her hands angrily. She decided to ring her father that night when the girls were in bed and invite herself and the girls down for the weekend; her cousin was a lawyer and lived nearby, might be a good sounding block too. Tomorrow she'd see about changing the locks on the doors to the house as a precautionary matter, but then she thought, would this be allowed? After all he still had rights to the house, or had he forfeited those rights with his behaviour? The more she turned over the problems, the more confused she became; she really did need advice.

After tea Helen and the girls went for a long walk with the dogs, they laughed and made up jokes as though nothing had happened to alter their way of life and happiness; as usual they'd taken a bag with them to pick blackberries and as usual, most were eaten by Sophie and the two Dachshunds, Charlotte and Helen laughing at their juice-covered faces, the daft old Great Dane tried valiantly to eat them but took in the leaves and thorns and spent minutes spitting them out, leaving him with bleeding lips, which Helen had to bathe when they returned home. As the day drew to a close and the early evening started, the girls splashed happily in the bath with the dogs trying to get in with them. Soon the smell of clean children enveloped Helen, and she vowed even more to protect her girls from all the traumas that might be ahead, never again would they be exposed to the horrors that she and Charlotte had heard this morning, happiness and normality must be restored as quickly as possible. It crossed Helen's mind that William would try and take the girls away from her, citing some unfounded lie of her neglect of the girls. She knew, from past experience of his cruelty, that he'd do anything to make her stay in the house as miserable as possible and try and drive her out; she knew too, that he'd never obey the law and taunt and abuse the rights of her and the children as much as possible. This frightened her and made her resolve even more finite.

With the girls in bed and asleep, Helen returned downstairs, preparatory to ringing her father and saw Bill, the barrister friend from the farm down the road, standing by the front door.

"Bill, how good to see you, come in, how's Pauline and the boys?"

"Fine, thanks, but I didn't come in with pleasantries, I'm much more concerned about you. We had a visit from your husband and his boyfriend earlier today, and I think I'd better get you some legal advice post haste. The pair of them have gone north for a few days, how long I don't know, but you need to be prepared for the worst." His face showed concern, so much so that Helen knew not to question but to listen. He continued, "Whatever you do, don't provoke him into doing something harmful to you and the girls. Have you made any plans yet?"

"No, not really, just practical ones. I know I must seek legal advice and I must divorce him as soon as possible. I don't want the girls too traumatised." Bill nodded in agreement, she continued, "I'd like to stay around here so as not to disturb the girls' education and for us not to lose our friends. I was thinking of getting in a locksmith tomorrow and putting better locks on the house, for security."

"Whatever you do, don't do that for the time being; don't go away or tell anyone what's happening until the divorce papers have been served and the case is underway. Take advice from the solicitors and only do as they tell you. Remember, William is extremely volatile, and you want him to make the mistakes, not you. Now tomorrow I've an old friend coming to stay, we have a case coming up, but his firm will be the firm for you to deal with, they have a very good record in matrimonial law. Do you mind if I give him your number and bring him down to see you tomorrow?"

"Not at all, I'd be delighted, it saves me trying to find someone reputable."

"Good, then we'll be here about five for an informal chat and you can give him some tea. I'll take the girls back with me and they can have their supper with our boys, Pauline will be delighted to have them, and you can follow on when you've finished talking and join us for dinner. Now, I'd better get back." He turned and looked at her gently, reassuring her with a touch on her arm. "Look, don't worry, in a year's time it'll all be over and a distant memory and a new life will have opened up for you and the girls."

He gave Helen a quick nod and grabbed his bicycle from the drive and after a wave disappeared home. The following day, Helen was registered with the law firm and a date was made for her to go and see them; she had to wait until the children were back at school but she had her date and knew what evidence she had to produce. For the next few days items were gathered and dates and comments written down carefully; each evening after the children were in bed, she meticulously went through the list, the items, the dates and comments. She dreaded William's coming back unexpectedly and particularly before her meeting, every knock on the door or every odd car on the track made her suspicious and she'd run upstairs to see who it was. She'd convinced the girls that whilst their father was 'away', it would be wise to keep the front door locked at all times and just play in the back garden and paddock with the dogs. Luckily, the weather was fine and warm, and they all made as much use as possible of the garden and paddling pool and the treat of eating outside.

The girls were due back at school the following Tuesday, so on the Saturday Helen planned to take them to the zoo, and on Sunday they were going to Pauline and Bill's for lunch; hopefully, *he'd* not appear over the weekend but Helen was wary and told Pauline and Bill of her fears. Pauline suggested that the girls stay over on the Sunday night, just in case anything happened, but she would leave the final choice to the girls. Helen agreed and Bill found the camp beds and collected some bedding and the girls' clothes from Helen. They said nothing to Charlotte and Sophie, preferring to keep it a surprise 'for the end of the holiday', as Bill said.

Saturday came and it was another lovely day, all Helen could think of was to get away quickly and safeguard the children and by ten o'clock, she and the two girls were in the little car on their way to the zoo; as they rounded each bend to the main road and no other car was there, Helen heaved a sigh of relief and the tension gradually subsided. The zoo was great fun and the girls were soon riding everything they could, and then they went to feed the animals in the children's zoo. Charlotte was a little more cautious but joined her sister and soon had a baby chimp clinging to her whilst Sophie was busily feeding an ant eater and a baby antelope that kept butting her. Helen decided to spend a long time with them in the little zoo and allowed them to feed the baby lambs and goats. She decided to finish the day with a meal at the zoo, and the girls were very excited at being allowed to eat anything they wanted to, and so an hour later, two very smelly and tired girls were in the car, clutching their books and crayons fast asleep, Helen didn't mind, they could stay up tonight and go to bed late; the nearer they got to home, the tighter the knot of fear in her stomach grew and the slower her driving became, she edged slowly around the final bend and the house loomed into view. 'Thank God, no lights and no car, we're safely back.' Helen turned into the drive and parked the car, she opened the door and went into each room, switching on the lights, half expecting to see him sitting in the dark, but, there really was no one there. Quietly, she unlocked the kennels and the dogs were immediately all over her and into the house, coming back outside to the car as two sleepy little heads emerged and went into the house, the dogs licking them and 'herding' them at every opportunity. Helen quickly shut the gate and went back into the house, carefully locking the door behind her; the girls had already gone upstairs with the dogs and she could hear laughter and mad 'scampers' as the girls ran the water for their baths and got ready for bed. Helen thought, 'They're tired, I wonder if they'll come down again or whether it'll be a story and sleep?' In a short time, the curtains were closed and the window locks double-checked, the dogs' food put down and Helen went upstairs to see to the girls. Two very sleepy faces greeted her, Charlotte was trying to wash her sister's hair but there was more shampoo on the dogs than on Sophie.

"I thought it'd help if I started washing Sophie's hair, it smells really bad but I'm not very good."

"My eyes hurt and Charlotte pulls my hair," moaned Sophie.

"Well, at least Charlotte tried and I think that's a real help. Did you enjoy today?"

The girls nodded and Helen laughed and wiped Sophie's eyes. Charlotte handed the shampoo over to her mother and proceeded to wash herself and try and wash her hair too, but it was impossible so that task was left to her mother; after another ten minutes the two girls were safely in bed cuddled up to their mother, listening to a story. Of course, tonight had to be about

33

animals and so an old book of Helen's was read, 'The Blue Elephant', sighs and questions were asked and gradually, Sophie dropped off to sleep with Charlotte following soon after. Helen kissed them both and quietly left the room, the two dachshunds following behind, all was peaceful.

The following day was bright and very warm, and the girls ran off down the road to see Bill and Pauline and the boys, leaving Helen to collect the items she was taking to the solicitor's on Tuesday that she wanted to show Bill; when she arrived, Pauline gave her a glass of wine and Bill started looking at the 'evidence'. Helen and Pauline continued preparing the food, chatting happily to each other.

"Well, you've really gone to town on this, good for you, it's exactly what's needed. Ben will be really pleased with this, it'll save him a lot of time in the preparation of the case. I think that this will go through quickly; after all, William no longer wants you and neither you him, so, I think 'unreasonable behaviour' and 'irreconcilable differences' will be all that's needed in mitigation. The only thing that I can see as being a stumbling block will be the house and contents."

"But surely, Helen will get the house, she's two children to look after, he's got to provide a roof over their heads." Pauline shook the saucepan with vigour and handed it to Helen to empty into a tureen.

"Now you know as well as I do that it doesn't work like that, the house will still have to be sold and it and the contents split fifty-fifty, but I'm sure with Helen automatically getting custody of the children, an easy compromise will be made. William's bound to get good advice on that one."

"Want a bet?" said Pauline, "You know how difficult he's been in the past on trivial matters, I bet he makes life for Helen hell and tries and prolongs the proceedings for as long as possible."

"He won't be able to do that, the lawyers will see to that, the one thing they can't abide is time wasters. However, you've a point and I'll mention it to Ben on Monday. Come on you lot, wash your hands, lunch is ready."

Four bright-eyed little faces careered into the kitchen and shot off to the cloakroom to do as they were told, reappearing eagerly and surveying the food in front of them. Lunch was delicious and the chatter animated, the day remained glorious, the three friends enjoyed each other's company and the children played happily together. All too soon it was time to go, and Helen and the girls waved and started down the road, dusk was falling, but Helen noticed a faint light ahead, immediately the knot of anxiety tightened, she held onto the children's hands firmly and at the turn in the track saw a light showing through a chink in the curtains. 'He's back,' she thought, 'now what do I do?' Charlotte squeezed her mother's hand, she'd noticed the light too.

"He's in the house!" she whispered, "I'll go back to see Uncle Bill and I'll take Sophie with me, our things are there and they said we could stay the night." She turned to her sister, "Come on, Sophie, race you back. I want to stay at the farm with the boys, and Uncle Bill and Auntie Pauline said we could."

Helen looked at her daughter, the child was so clever at assessing situations and realising a solution.

"Yes do, ask Uncle Bill that if I haven't been in touch in the next half an hour, to please ring me."

Charlotte took her sister's protesting hand and quickly ran back to the house. Helen watched till they reached the gate and waved to her, she waved back and then with a heavy heart went through the gate and into the house; he was standing in front of the fireplace in the hall and glared at her.

"Where've you been and where are the girls? It's well past their bed-time and I came to see them. Don't suppose you've fed them, and I want some dinner too, I've driven a long way and I'm tired and I'm staying the night." After a pause he sneered back at her and said sarcastically, "After all, this is still my home or had you forgotten?"

"The girls are staying the night with Bill and Pauline and we've all eaten, they invited us for lunch and tea. If you like, I'll cook something for you now."

Helen tried to be flippant and friendly at the same time, but her heart was thumping against her ribs as she wondered what his next move would be. She smiled at him, he glowered back and raised his hand as if to hit her; she winced but never moved, he ran his hand through his hair in frustration.

"Well, they'll be looked after there, which is more than I can say for their staying here. I suppose you've been telling your friends what an animal I am and turning people against me."

Helen looked at him with pity, his pent up anger intense, and said, "No, I've said nothing to anyone, just that you're away. Bill knows that we have a problem, nothing more."

He moved closer to her and clenched his fist, she waited for the smack, nothing came, and instead he retreated and rubbed his hands and spoke more quietly and defensively.

"I've decided I'm not going to stay," suddenly a mood swing as he turned to her snarling, "This house is filthy and I know there's not much in the fridge, I've already looked."

"Perhaps you could leave me some money, then I could stock up the fridge and you could stay."

"Why, if you want money, ask your father, and as for food, nothing you give me will be good enough." He became heated and shook his finger at her, "I'll give you nothing, I'll see you back in the gutter, where I found you and where you belong. Oh, and I intend to fight for the custody of the girls, so don't try any funny business; I mean to leave you with nothing and deprive you of everything."

With that he lunged for the door and slammed it shut behind him. Helen stood in the hall shaking, the old Great Dane came up beside her and nuzzled her hand, the other two stood cowering in the kitchen doorway; the phone rang, it was Bill.

"Can you speak, monosyllables will do if it's difficult. We gather William came back, are you all right? The girls are in bed and asleep."

"Yes, I can, and yes, he did, but he's gone now. It was awful and before I forget, I must write everything he said down before I see Ben."

"Good girl, you're learning. I presume he wants everything, including the girls, and is going to leave you with nothing. It's the sort of behaviour I rather suspected would happen but not quite so soon. Homosexuals can either be very kind and compassionate, or like him, malevolent and cruel. Don't worry, he may try to get everything but he won't succeed, you also have rights. One thing he'll never be allowed is custody of the girls, but he'll try with lies to get them."

"I'm afraid knowing him he'll find a way to succeed. It's now 1976 and anything's possible. Anyway, the gloves are off and I know what to expect. Thank you so much for keeping the girls overnight, I hope they're not too upset, I'll try and make the last day of the holidays a fun day. Good night and thank Pauline for the lovely lunch and tea, it really was delicious. I have the dogs, so all's well here."

The phone clicked and all was silent again. Helen opened the front door just to make sure he'd gone and locked the gate, the dogs running around the garden not wanting to leave her. Once safely inside she went into the sitting-room and collapsed into a chair, her legs giving way beneath her; this had been a shock, probably the first of many, she had to keep her wits about her and remain calm.

Pauline arrived on the doorstep at nine o'clock the following morning with the girls and the boys, and Helen made breakfast for them all. She was still 'shell-shocked' from the confrontation the night before and had had little sleep, constantly waking at the slightest noise outside, twice the Great Dane had grunted and padded down the corridor to the stairs, but after an 'hurrumph' had returned to the bedroom and settled down.

"You look all in," said Pauline, "no doubt sleep evaded you somewhat. I'm afraid you may have many nights like that in the future before this awful business is over."

"I know, it really wasn't pleasant, and I'm so glad the girls were with you both. I don't know what he'd have done if he'd seen them." Helen proceeded to tell Pauline what had happened and by the time the story had been recounted, she began to feel stronger in herself and to instinctively know how to deal with a similar situation in the future. "Perhaps I'll grow 'into it' and know how to deal with situations as they arise," she said. Pauline looked at her friend and helped put the bacon and eggs on the plates for the children.

"Rather you than me; come on all of you, breakfast's ready." As fast as they came in and ate, they were gone back into the sunshine, clutching half-eaten toast and apples, happy as crickets with not a care in the world.

"How I wish everyday was like this for them. I've got an awfully big field to furrow and I do wonder how straight the lines are going to be. I'll be honest with you, Pauline, I'm frightened, scared rigid would be a better description, I'm dreading tomorrow and apprehensive about the outcome. What if he comes back and takes a knife to me again, what on earth do I do?" Genuine disquiet was etched on her face, and Pauline pitied her but spoke reassuringly.

"It won't come to anything like that, he wouldn't dare, besides he knows he wants you out of his life, so the sooner it gets going the sooner it's finished and you can both get on with your separate lives. You've just got to remain positive and take all the 'flack' in your stride. Remember, we're only down the road and will always be around when you need a shoulder to cry on."

"Thanks Pauline, you're a brick; it's nice to know, in a way, I'm not alone." The two friends cleared away, locked the house and took the dogs and children for a walk over the hill. It was a beautiful day, none of them wanted to be parted from each other and so they returned to the house for more food and play, with Helen and Pauline sitting in the garden, the former sewing name tabs onto the girls' uniforms.

"Charlotte and I have decided to open a sweet shop, what do you think, Mum?" said a tousle-headed boy to his mother.

"Very good idea, when do you intend doing this and how much is it going to cost?" the ever-practical Pauline gazed at her son.

"Oh, I don't know," he scratched his head, "I suppose in about five years' time, oh and I thought you and Dad could fund it just until it was making a profit. Charlotte and I think it's a brilliant idea, so I'm going to study business and Charlotte's going to study law; we'll make a fortune."

He disappeared to find the others, and Pauline and Helen laughed, "Well, at least they're sorted," said Pauline, they continued talking awhile until Pauline looked at her watch, "Oh heck, I forgot the time, I must break up the party and go and make sure the boys have all their kit for school before Bill gets home. Let us know how you get on tomorrow, we'll be thinking of you."

"Thanks, I will."

Pauline and the boys parted at the gate, and soon Helen, Charlotte and Sophie had everything for school in the proper bags, ready for the next day. They had their usual end of holidays 'special' tea, this time in the garden, the dogs trying hard to lick the plates and generally eat anything that was left over. After long baths and stories, the girls were soon fast asleep, dreaming happily. Helen returned to her briefcase for one final check and then went for a walk around the garden in the warm dusk; bees were buzzing in the late flowers and butterflies flitted about in the sedum, the year's lambs settled down against the fence for the night and the swallows gathered overhead on the telephone wires whilst the dogs ambled about in the bushes or settled at her feet. It was all so peaceful and bucolic, how could the awful events of the summer really be true, would some miracle happen and it all go away? No, it was real and no, it wouldn't go away, but soon, one day in the future, another evening like this would happen; she'd be wiser, the girls would be more grown up and the events of the last weeks would be a foul and distant memory; but for the time being she must protect and keep the girls happy, get the divorce over and themselves settled into another place and their lives renewed…tomorrow was another day and she looked forward to it with hope.

Chapter 4

The chaos of the first day back to school exploded on their senses like fireworks; as usual Charlotte had too many books and not enough sports clothes in her bag, and Sophie got to school having forgotten her homework of the holidays. Helen promised to bring it to the school later on, but now all she wanted to do was to settle the girls and disappear to her meeting with the solicitors. She drove out of the school gates and made her way into the town, her appointment with destiny making her more positive and alive. She rounded the corner of the High Street and soon found the offices of 'Turners and Sons'; she couldn't miss it, it was an imposing late Victorian house covered in ivy and full of grand carvings. She went up the steps and knocked on the imposing black front door with its heavy brass furniture and was soon ushered into reception. Ten minutes later she was seated in a grand office with Ben Turner and his secretary Mrs Blois, she with notepad and pen, Helen with a cup of tea and a box of tissues in front of her. The 'evidence' was laid out before her, the pass book, her notebook, a tube of KY jelly and two pairs of differing underpants; a shaft of sunlight came through the high windows and illuminated it all. Suddenly she felt nausea overcome her in waves and saw herself in this scenario as dirty; she panicked and drank her tea, what had she started, how would it end, what would happen later when he found out?

After the pleasantries had been exchanged and the general format of the proceedings had been explained, Ben and his secretary carefully reviewed the notebooks and pass books she'd laid out for him; he turned to her, the pass book in his hand, "Did you really not know about this and how much was in it before you found it?"

"No, I didn't," she replied. "There were others in the glove box of the car, and I've noted their contents in the little notebook

40

on the table, but I wanted you to see what they were like so that you'd believe me, that's why I kept one. I've got to try and return the one in your hand, without his knowing, back to the car when he comes back, and he will once he misses it."

"Hmm, I understand, but didn't you know how much was in these pass books? Surely, after all these years of marriage you must have had an idea."

"No, Mr Turner, I didn't. I know it'll seem strange to you but I am speaking the truth. I used to have a monthly allowance from him for food and small household items, nothing more, this he paid into my bank account at the beginning of each month. If I wanted anything else, that is clothes or special treats for the girls, I had to ask him for the money and then give the receipts and any spare cash back to him. He would fill up my car each week and take a note of the mileage and then question me if I'd 'gone too far' and I'd have to explain; I'm afraid I've not been able to find that book. So you see, because I was so carefully monitored, I had no reason to question him and just thought it normal; it's only now with your questioning that I'm beginning to realise that I've been 'conned', with everything having to be asked for. At the time, knowing his behaviour to me, I didn't dare step 'out of line' nor question anything."

"Yes, I can see that now," he put the books down on the table and picked up the KY jelly. "I suppose you know what this is for?"

"Yes a friend told me." Her hands twisted in her lap with embarrassment, the knot of sordid dirt and hurt tightened in her stomach.

"And I suppose the switch from conventional to, shall we say, 'slimmer' pants happened recently too."

"About six months ago, I started to notice a change," Helen said, whilst trying to keep her eyes averted from Ben and stare at the table.

Ben returned everything to the table and carefully checked Mrs Blois' notes. To them all this preparation was quite normal, the minutes ticked by; to Helen it was a nightmare, she felt as if her entire life was under scrutiny.

Ben looked up from the secretary's notes and said, "I think you could do with a break, let's have some more tea. Mrs Blois, would you be so kind?" She picked up the tray with a smile and disappeared out of the door.

"Look, I know this is very painful for you, but if we can get all this preliminary work done thoroughly now, then it won't seem so bad later on. You're doing well and what you've prepared for me today is excellent it'll make a huge difference in the presenting of our case to the other side. Now, before Mrs Blois comes back with the tea, I have to ask you two very personal questions. Firstly, have you ever been unfaithful to him?"

"No, never, after his behaviour I'm not interested in other men, and doubt I ever will be again."

"Yes, I can see that, but we're not *all* like that, you know. You've had a very nasty experience." He smiled kindly at her before continuing, "My second question is a little harder. Before you answer, listen to what I have to say; it may be that the other side, in mitigation, will argue that his present 'affair' is just a fling due to difficulties in business and that now he sees the hurt he's caused, he wishes to make amends for the wrongs he's done to you and the girls. In some cases like this one, where there is an awkward situation, it's not unknown for couples to live together in harmony despite there being a 'ménage à trois'. I'm sorry to have to ask you but it's necessary. If he were to come back and resume marital relations, would you accept him?"

Helen felt her fury over the last eleven years start to well up inside her, the injustices she'd suffered and the unhappiness of her lost youth flooded over her; she breathed deeply and the anger subsided and common sense returned. She said calmly,

"I definitely don't want him back, and as to so-called 'marital relations' that's a joke, those have been missing for several years. I've been celibate since Sophie was born, he's tried but then looked at me with revulsion and immediately stopped."

"Good, that's exactly what I wanted to hear, I'm sorry I had to ask you such a personal question. Thank you for answering it so calmly, I know it must have been very hard. Ah, here's Mrs Blois with the tea." Ben stood and took the tray from her and set it down on the table and poured, once this had been done and the tea handed around, he resumed, "I've a few more questions to ask you, and then you can go and we'll get on with sending the papers out."

For the next hour Helen's life and her feelings and thoughts were tossed around like so many pieces of confetti, one question after another, counter questioning and then response, until her head was spinning and she began to question her own answers, were they correct, had she missed anything, were the timings of incidents right?

Soon it was over and Ben was standing up shaking hands with her, "Now don't you worry, I'm quite sure that this will go through smoothly and then you and your ex can restart your lives anew. It's quite an easy case really, neither of you wants the other, so provided you both take the advice of your respective solicitors, and provided neither of you is difficult over the division of assets etc., then I can see no reason why the decree nisi can't be granted before Christmas, with the absolute a mere formality six weeks later. Payments to yourself and the girls shouldn't be difficult either; as you're working, we'll be concentrating on the maintenance for the girls. I'm afraid where you're concerned it'll be difficult to get anything for you, you must understand this and try not to be greedy but allow us to guide you."

"I understand, and anyway, it's the girls I'm more anxious about, making sure I can support them, I've had nothing from him for at least a month and been living on overdraft."

"Hmm, Mrs Blois, make a note to apply for an affidavit for an immediate financial breakdown of William Sands' bank accounts, Mrs Sands and the girls cannot be left with nothing. Let's see if we can't get an interim payment for you." He smiled and with another shake of the hand, she was dismissed.

Mrs Blois saw her to the door and the freedom of the outside world. Helen stood on the doorstep, drawing in great lungsful of fresh air and blinked at the sunlight. Suddenly, she was happy for the first time in years, genuinely happy, she felt that a great burden had been lifted from her shoulders and someone else was dealing with her problems. She almost 'danced' back to her car and then stopped, she'd have lunch in the little town in celebration. Across from the car was a tea room called 'The Old Wheel,' it looked quaint and 'olde-worlde', it would do. She walked inside and it was as she'd hoped, old beams and smoke-stained walls; she found a free table in the bay window and settled down. Within seconds a sullen but pretty faced girl chewing gum came across, Helen surveyed her,

"Taste nice?"

"What?" came the reply.

"Your gum."

"Oh yes, tasteless now though, excuse me," She turned slightly away and removed the gum and put it in her pocket, "Now then, what do you want? By the way, I'm Deirdre." It was obvious to Helen that there'd be no menu and that Deirdre had no intention of even looking for one, so she said she'd like coffee and a sandwich if it were possible, "You can have ham, egg and cress or chicken salad," came the reply.

Helen opted for the chicken salad, then she asked, remembering the 'gum' incident, "Do you prepare the food yourself?"

"Oh no, that's my brother, he's a trainee chef, quite good, even if I do say so myself." With that Deirdre disappeared into the back to deliver the order. Helen watched her go and looked out of the window at the people scurrying about. She decided she'd take the dogs, after their walk, with her in the car to pick up the girls, they always loved seeing them and she didn't care that the car would be covered in dog hairs, that was natural and normal and from now on everything would be as 'normal' as possible. She looked around at the tiny café, the dingy smoke-covered walls and grimy pictures and thought, 'This must have been nice in a bygone era, when scones, home-made cakes and delicious coffee were served to a plethora of suitably suited and hatted clientele, and where manners and decency were the *norm*.' Now the place was faded and unloved and living on its memories.

Deirdre reappeared with her coffee and food, Helen was amazed, her sandwich and coffee were beautifully presented unlike the lackadaisical Deirdre, who served everything as quickly as possible before disappearing back to the kitchen and her brother. Helen settled down to eat and didn't notice the distinguished looking man in the other window. She finished quickly and got up to leave, failing to realise that her bag, which was open, was resting on her skirt; with a clatter the contents fell to the floor, plus the 'evidence' she'd had with her in the solicitor's office. As she bent down she noticed the various eyes staring at her and refilled her bag quickly, stuffing everything willy-nilly into it and checking that the 'evidence' was safely stowed away. She walked over to pay her bill; she pressed the bell on the counter and Deirdre reappeared and was again chewing gum.

"Everything all right, was it?"

"Yes thank you, just what I needed."

"Good, see you again soon."

'Not if I can help it,' thought Helen; just as she turned to leave, she felt a light tap on her shoulder, it was the man from the other bay, his blue eyes twinkled.

"Excuse me, but I think you dropped these." He held up her car keys.

"Heavens, I'd have been lost without those, thank you. Now I must go and get the children." He held the door open for her, and they stood and momentarily gazed at each other, "Goodbye, and thank you again for finding my keys."

"Not at all, let's hope I can help again one day, you looked lost in thought, goodbye."

"Yes, I'm afraid I was, goodbye."

He turned and walked down the street, she returned to the car and the road home. A thought crossed her mind, 'Would he be there?' surely not was the reply, today's a working day. She relaxed and in no time was at the house collecting the dogs, who were anxious for their walk. She thought about her meeting and decided not to tell the children anything but wait until she received the outcome and replies to the letters being sent out. Walks over and the dogs in the car, Helen was soon at the school, she was met by Charlotte's form mistress.

"Mrs Sands, I wonder if I might have a word with you before you pick up the girls."

"Certainly, what's the matter?"

"I'm a little worried about Charlotte, she seems very tired. Is she sleeping well or is anything bothering her?"

Helen swallowed hard, this was just what she didn't need, and she decided that she'd dismiss it and have words with the solicitor in the morning as to whether she should inform the school. She smiled back and said,

"I think it may be the onset of puberty that's all, she is nearly twelve and she's been rushing around doing a lot of things during the holidays, she's probably come back to school for a rest!" the mistress's face fell, so Helen decided to tone her flippancy down. "But I'll have a word with the doctor and see what she says."

"Thank you so much, she's usually so lively in class."

Charlotte and Sophie appeared through the door and greeted their mother. Helen noticed that Charlotte did look a bit 'peaky', she put her arm around her, "Are you all right, you look a little tired."

"Yes, I'm fine, I'm a bit hungry, didn't like lunch very much and left it." She smiled up at her mother and ran to the car and the dogs, who were delighted to see her. Helen watched her go and thought 'Growing pains I suppose, it's about time; she'll be fine tomorrow.' She got into the driver's seat, looked at the girls again and quickly left the school for home; the usual chatter ensued with Sophie being the main chatterbox, the dogs curled up beside her and Charlotte.

Once home, the girls were soon into their homework whilst Helen prepared tea. Charlotte seemed much better and kept asking when tea was going to be ready, Helen said that she was "going as fast as she could, it'd be ready when you've finished your homework". There were further grumbles but soon tea was on the table and the girls ate ravenously and then asked to be excused from the table to go and play with the dogs. As Helen was clearing away, the phone rang; it was William.

"I've decided to come down on Saturday and see the girls, I'm taking them out for the day and then we'll talk, so whatever you've got planned cancel it, I come first. I'll be there at about ten o'clock, make sure the girls are ready." The phone clicked, silence filled the room. Helen thought, 'He can't know anything yet but he will by Saturday, what do I do now and will he bring John? Let's hope he does, at least there'll be no scenes.'

Charlotte came in through the door and sat down heavily.

"Do you mind if I go to bed now? I fancy a bath and an early night, I'm tired and I'd like to read my book."

"No, of course, you can go up, I think an early night's a good thing. Sophie can carry on playing for a little while. Do you want a hot drink later on?"

"Yes, can I have some hot chocolate, please?" She disappeared out of the kitchen, and Helen watched with slight concern, she'd see how she was in the morning. When the girls were in bed, Helen went over the events of the day and decided that she would ring Ben and seek his advice about the school and about allowing the children out with their father on Saturday. It was normal for him to want to see them and he had every right to do so, it just felt wrong to allow him near them so soon after he'd left, particularly if he brought John with him, how would people view two young girls out with two older men? It may be 1976 but to see two gays out together with two children was still an odd sight.

The following morning she rang Ben Turner, he listened quietly and after a short pause advised her to tell the headmaster of the little school and for her to tell the form teacher; as for her 'husband', there was nothing that could be done, she must let them go he was their father and entitled by law to see them; still, he'd be grateful if she'd ring him to say how it all went on the Monday and also to make arrangements for the house to go on the market; after all, she must be seen to be doing 'the right thing' and being co-operative.

On the Saturday morning the girls were ready to go out promptly at a quarter to ten, and Sophie was looking out of the window straining to see her father's car, Charlotte was more thoughtful and held back. Luckily, there had been no re-occurrence of the 'tiredness' episode and the child had been eager to go to school each morning, a happy face returning each afternoon full of what she'd done and learnt that day. Today, though, she hung back and looked intently at her mother.

"Do I have to go? I'd far rather stay at home with you and the dogs. I'd enjoy being quiet in the house and not have Sophie around me all the time. Can't I stay and go for a walk with you and the dogs?"

Helen looked at the upturned face, etched with misgiving, "I'm afraid not, I think it'd be good for you to go out somewhere different with him. You'll be home by six at the latest and then we've got all day tomorrow to go for a walk and have our own fun here. Do it, this once, for me, will you? If you really don't like it, I'll arrange something else more suitable for you, but this first time, try it out." Charlotte nodded but still kept hold of Helen's hand.

Sophie suddenly saw the car and came rushing back to them both, "He's here, Mummy, he's here. Come on, Charlotte, let's go and get in the car, bye see you later." Sophie stood on tiptoes and kissed her mother, Charlotte did likewise and reluctantly followed her sister to the waiting car.

"Hello you two, get in the back and sit still," he turned to Helen without leaving the car, "I'll be back at five, I'll speak to you then, you listen hard as I have to return home and it's a long journey to Coventry, I might be earlier, so be here." He turned the car around and disappeared with his precious cargo back down the track. 'So that's where you're living, is it? Nice of you to let me know,' Helen, with a last look at the diminishing dust, turned and went into the house. The day passed quietly, she went up to the little town and posted letters and shopped, then went home in case he was really early. She took the dogs for a short walk in the fields opposite, well within sight of the house, picked some blackberries and returned and waited; she knew there'd be an uproar when he got back. She laid a tray for tea and put out a fruit cake that had always been a favourite of his in their past life and made sandwiches for the girls' tea, in case their lunch had been bad, and waited.

Five o'clock came and went and she began to panic. She rang her father, he calmed her down and then asked for the registration number of the car, "Don't worry, love, I can have him stopped, you forget I've got contacts. If he's not back by seven, ring me again." She saw the lights of the car as she put the phone down, the car slewed to a stop, gravel being thrown up against the porch and windows.

"Come on, girls, we're home again, time for you to get out and go to bed." He opened the door, and two little figures got out silently and went into the house.

"Mummy, what's for tea?" they chorused.

"Well, there are some sandwiches but if you're really hungry, how about sausages and scrambled eggs?"

"I just want sandwiches," said Charlotte and Sophie nodded in agreement.

"Then take them with you and watch some television whilst your mother and I talk," said their father. They picked up their food and scuttled off to put on a favourite programme. "Now, you and I can talk." She followed him into the sitting-room and waited for the onslaught. "I've had the papers from my solicitors and they seem in order. I'm going to take some of the better things back with me tonight; I've decided to stay and do some clearing up of my possessions rather than leave you to 'steal' from me as I know you will. Remember, you own nothing, everything's been provided by me, and you'll just get the bare essentials the law says I have to leave for you and the girls. I've taken advice, you understand, don't you?"

She looked him straight in the eye. "Yes," she replied coldly, "take whatever you want, I'm sure John will be delighted with what you take back to your new home."

"You're right, he is my new home, and the house is beautiful," he paused and looked at her, making sure that the barb had found its mark, before carrying on. Helen's face remained immobile, nothing showed, he continued, "This place is nothing but a pigsty that you're living in. I'd never come back to this, I'd dare not show my new friends what it's like, they're county people, it's so filthy." He again looked at her, again she remained passive. "My solicitor suggested I give you fifty pounds, but I've decided on thirty, no doubt you'll manage. You see, I've another home to contribute to now," he said sarcastically.

"I hope that you will still help with the bills here; surely, you'll not see your children cold and hungry now the autumn's here."

"Oh, I'll make sure I do my part. I'll make arrangements with the bank to pay half, but you can find the rest."

"You know that'll be difficult, I can only work part-time until the girls are over eleven!"

"Well, that's your problem, you'll just have to solve it."

With that he started packing up pictures and porcelain and putting the items into boxes and carrying them to the car. Helen decided to help and enjoyed seeing the back of his so-called 'luxury items'; she started to feel slightly euphoric seeing 'precious items' go.

"As the house is on the market, I'll trust you not to do anything with the rest, I'll collect them later when it's sold." He disappeared to find the girls and say goodbye, then came back and strode past Helen and left.

The phone rang, it was her father, "Thought I'd give you a ring to see how things are going, also, your mother and I thought you'd like to come down at the weekend. Come Friday after school and stay until Sunday afternoon, it'll give the girls a break, and you and I can have a good talk. There's a theatre group coming to the Church Hall on Saturday afternoon and your mother thought she'd take the girls so they could let off some steam."

"Sounds like a plan, and we'd love to come, and 'yes' I'd love to have a good talk with you. See you both at about seven o'clock, I'll feed them first before we come, and then they can have time with you both before bed. It'll be so good to get away from this place. I've got people coming to look at the house on Saturday, but the agent can do that, I'll ring them tomorrow."

"Fine, won't talk now, all news at the weekend." She rang off and went to tell the girls and kiss them goodnight.

Chapter 5

Helen stirred in her dreams and watched as her daughter came in and stoked the fire and put the guard around it; she smiled up at her as Sophie gently put a rug over her mother's knees.

"Thank you, dear, do you want me to get up or can I have another ten minutes?"

"You're fine, have as long as you like, Ian's not home yet. Would you like a drink?"

"No thanks, not at the moment, I'm too comfortable where I am to move. I'm enjoying being lazy, I hope you don't mind."

"Not at all, stay where you are, I'll wake you later." Sophie gave a little pat to her mother's rug and left the room. Helen snuggled down, grateful for the peace and quiet; she looked at the fire and thought she saw her father smiling at her, 'Do you remember the dragons who lived in the caves in the fire when you were young? Charlotte had names for them all, she called them the Groats, she would tell tales about them to Sophie, who'd sit transfixed cuddling her bear, and yes, she talks about the Groats even now to your mother and I.' Helen blinked and sat staring into the fire, willing her father to return, but he didn't, it was just another figment of her imagination, her memories, but she did remember the dragon's caves; she smiled and her eyes closed again...

"Crumpets," said Helen's mother, "that's what we need, crumpets running with butter and honey, that'll warm us up when we get home. Mummy will have made tea for us all. Wasn't it kind of Bill and Pauline to have the dogs? They'd be frozen in this. Come on, best foot forward and let's think of a word and tell a story around it." She tucked Sophie's reluctant hand into her own and willed the child to walk faster to keep the cold at bay. It was starting to snow and the flakes were settling on their noses. Charlotte was valiantly trying to catch them with her tongue, her grandfather tickling her when she tried and making her laugh, so they went down her throat.

"I'm so cold, Grandma, I can't feel my feet and my knees hurt," moaned Sophie, snuggling nearer to her grandmother's coat, "can't we stop for a while?"

Her grandmother looked at the tired upturned face and put her arm around the child and held her close, "I'm afraid not, dear, if we do that you'll freeze like a statue and all the little animals will try and get into your pockets for warmth." It did the trick, Sophie's imagination ran riot and she walked beside her grandmother with renewed vigour, asking question after question about the animals and which ones would get into her coat and which she'd take home and keep. "Oh, knowing you, all of them, but I don't think we'd better keep the little mice as Pussy will eat them and that wouldn't be very nice, would it?" Sophie agreed with that and started chattering about what food they'd all need and where they could be put safely in the garden to keep warm. Charlotte and her grandfather joined them both and soon whilst talking, laughing and sliding down the hill, they were at the front door and home.

Helen greeted them all and after the initial chatter and dis-robing of the children, followed them into her parents' drawing-room and the fire. Her father rubbed his hands and stood by the fire and the girls sat on the rug, looking for the 'dragons' in the 'caves'; the cat came and nestled up against Sophie, it too, looking into the fire, Sophie stroked it. Grandma handed Charlotte a crumpet on the end of a long fork and showed her how to toast it in the fire whilst Helen went back to the kitchen to bring in the tea trolley; eventually, Charlotte and her grandmother had managed to toast six crumpets and Sophie had in that time eaten two; her chin now covered in melted butter, she grinned up at them all, "I like crumpets, they're great!"

"Grandma, when can I have a crumpet? Sophie's eaten mine, and I'm hungry too," moaned Charlotte, glaring at her sister.

"Right now, you can have two as well, but you can have strawberry jam on yours because you helped me, and Grandpa can have the other two."

"What about Mummy and you, Grandma? You've got nothing," chirped Sophie, putting her sticky hand on top of her mother's hand.

"That's all right," said Grandma, "we've got a sandwich instead."

"Can I have strawberry jam on a sandwich, please Mummy, please I'll eat it all, really I will, I promise." Her mother nodded and the child had her sandwich, the jam happily mixing with the melted butter on her chin. She turned back to the fire and her sister and the cat, and they all continued to look for the 'dragons' in the fire.

Tea carried on and the girls talked about the snow starting and how cold it became, and the worry of what would happen to the animals, would they be all right during the night, and Grandpa promising to help the girls make little 'homes' in the garden just in case they wanted a different home.

"You'll have to put leaves and moss inside for warmth, and we'll see if there are any nuts and currants in the larder that Grandma can give us for them."

Two pairs of large eyes looked imploringly at their grandmother, "How could I possibly refuse, whilst you're in bed tonight, I'll see what I can find." The two excited faces smiled broadly at her before turning back to the fire and chattering animatedly to each other.

Helen and her parents continued to drink tea and talk, Helen recounting all the events of the last week and the solicitor's advice, William's sudden appearance to take the girls out for the day and his taking of some of their possessions. This last revelation shocked her mother but not her father, as Helen said, "They're nothing but inanimate objects; they're not human and precious like the girls."

"I know that," said her mother, "but they still make a home and some of the things he's taken you were fond of and had learnt about."

"I know, but, actually, it's something less for me to worry about. He's promised not to take anything else until the house is sold. He's only taken little 'bits', and I'm not worried about them, the place looks more spacious; one thing I am grateful to him for taking though is that pair of awful faience figures on the plinths in the dining-room; do you remember them, ghastly things. I kept hoping that one of the dogs would knock them over and smash them, but they never did. Anyway, they've now gone along, with a couple of pictures which were his mother's and I

53

always hated, so badly painted, and the little boxes on the window ledge in the drawing-room."

"Thank heavens those figures have gone," said her mother laughing, "they cluttered up that dining-room dreadfully, and I agree with you they were ghastly, so vulgar, should have been on a fair ground."

"Well, his final words when he left were, 'that he'd leave the rest until the house was sold and collect later, trusting me not to 'steal' anything," Helen said in mimicry of her husband's tone.

"How kind of him," her mother said sarcastically, "so long as he doesn't take the things you've inherited."

"I don't think he'd dare, he may be a bully but he's also a coward, and the one thing he won't do is flout the law," said Helen.

"Don't be too sure of that, that man has the cunning of the devil; he'll not get his hands dirty, he'll leave that to someone else," said her father. "You forget I've had the odd business dealing with him in the past, remember the cars? My eyes were opened to one or two things on more than one occasion due to overheard conversations in his office. He never did anything underhand with your mother and I, but it was obvious things did happen, so be on your guard, Helen, be very careful with him indeed."

The room fell silent as the three of them became immersed in their own thoughts; Helen was definitely apprehensive about the outcome, always had been, her father had just voiced her innermost thoughts. Her mother's thoughts were jumbled, no cohesive logic emerging from anything, seeing everything as an awful dream. She looked from her daughter to her husband for some 'sign' but there was nothing, just deep scowls. Helen's father was deep in thought too, he could see this whole escapade turning into a terrible disaster if it wasn't handled with care. He knew William was slightly 'unhinged' by the whole process, but he, he didn't care about; it was his daughter and granddaughters he was more concerned with, how to protect them. He decided to quietly talk to a barrister friend of his in his Lodge, see what advice he'd give if anything went wrong suddenly; he'd say nothing to Helen, only if and when it became necessary.

Helen and her father were woken from their reveries by her mother's offer of 'more tea', each of them declined and Helen took the trolley into the kitchen. She heard her mother tell the children to come to the table and have a game of 'snakes and ladders' before bedtime. She listened to the whoops of glee from the girls and started putting things away and into the dish washer; the cat meandered in and rubbed itself comfortingly against her leg.

"I know, it's time for your food, just wait a minute." She picked up the cat and nuzzled into its warm fur and listened to the deep purr, the cat rubbed affectionately against her face and gave a little mew of impatience, she put her down. "All right, I'll feed you, I know your affection's just cupboard love." The cat mewed again with pleasure and rubbed even harder until her food was in front of her, then forgot Helen in the pleasure of devouring it. Helen finished clearing away and turned to leave the room; the cat had finished feeding and was now sitting primly cleaning itself, it stopped looked at her and quietly disappeared through the cat-flap and into the snow, Helen returned to her family.

The game of 'snakes and ladders' was in full swing when Helen returned to the drawing-room,

"Whatever you do, don't speak," said her father tersely, "this daughter of yours is beating me and I don't like it, I never lose!"

Sophie giggled and watched intently as Charlotte and their Grandfather battled it out together, she and her grandmother were so far behind, forever falling down the ladders, it didn't really matter what happened to them; the other two were arch rivals and ignoring everyone in their bid to win. Helen sat quietly between them all and watched and tried to help Sophie and her mother but to no avail, they were all too engrossed in the battle going on between Charlotte and her grandfather. The dice flew all over the place and the snakes were slithered up and down and the ladders run up and down too and so the game went on, until there was a 'whoop' of joy from Charlotte, she'd won.

"You cheated, you should have come down, not gone up, you were there." Grandfather pointed to a space with indignation.

Charlotte smiled back at him. "No, I didn't, Grandpa, you weren't concentrating."

Grandfather grumbled good-naturedly and said, "Girls today are too clever for their own good," and then, "What about a drink before bedtime and a marshmallow?" Squeals of delight came from the girls, and they ran out of the room with their grandfather chattering away to him as they went.

"Heavens, that was fun," said her mother, "but I'm afraid I was no use to Sophie at all."

"Never mind, she obviously enjoyed watching and playing, and that's all part of the game, isn't it? I shouldn't worry too much, they've all had a good time."

The girls returned with their drinks and the cat and sat in front of the fire, looking again for the 'dragons'; her father poured out drinks for herself and her mother and came back to his chair with his. All was peaceful and Helen wondered if this was the calm before the storm, but she'd talk later when the girls were asleep. However, it was not to be, their peace was broken by the phone ringing in the hall; her father groaned and her mother wondered "Who it could be?" and Helen said she'd go and see.

"Tell them I'll ring in the morning," her father called to her.

"All right," said Helen. "Hello, who's there?"

"Helen, is that you? I'm so glad. It's Jill here from the farm. I just think you ought to know that I think William's in the house emptying it, there's a small removal van in the garden. Eddie's been down and spoken to a man, who says he's your brother-in-law, he's called Jack, is that right? Eddie said he was very embarrassed and said he'd been asked to help. I said I'd give you a ring as I knew where you were and leave you to deal with things."

"You're quite right, and, yes, Jack is my brother-in-law; this'll be the work of my sister-in-law, Jack's wife. She's always been a vindictive bitch and hated what William and I have collected over the years, but don't worry, as far as I'm concerned, they're welcome to everything, I've got the most precious items and they're here safe and well and having fun with their grandparents."

"I knew you'd say that, but even so, it's a cowardly act, but I suppose, typical of him to do this when he knew you'd be away."

"Yes, it's the nature of the beast, and I'd half expected it but not quite yet. I've got a number for my solicitor, so I'll give him a ring and take his advice. Thanks so much for telling me, I'll be home tomorrow late afternoon, so tell Eddie to have a pitch-fork handy just in case!"

Jill laughed. "I promise I'll do that, just take care, but if I were you, I'd give school a miss for the girls on Monday and come back that afternoon, at least no one will be here then."

"Good idea, but half of me wants to come back tomorrow and give him and any others a thick ear if I catch any of them red-handed. I must put the girls to bed now and then I'll talk to my father tonight, after I've spoken with the solicitor."

"OK, but don't even think about coming home tomorrow, take the easy option; take care and we'll be looking out for you on Monday. Bye."

"Bye and thanks." Helen replaced the receiver as her father emerged from the drawing-room.

"Problems?"

"Yes, bad ones; stay and listen whilst I make one more phone call, then I won't have to repeat myself." Helen dialled the number, her father waited by her side.

The phone was answered at the other end, "Hello, is that you Ben? I'm sorry to disturb you on a Saturday night, but I need some advice. William's at the house with his brother-in-law emptying it, my neighbour from the farm has just phoned me. Her husband's been down and seen that there's a removal van in the drive and spoken to my brother-in-law, who says he's been asked to help clear the house." A pause and talking at the other end, "No, I'd rather not go home, I'm with the girls and staying with my parents. I'd rather keep everything as normal as possible whilst here, and return to the mess on Monday." More talking from the other end and then an end to conversation as the phone was replaced.

"Well, Dad, you were right, the worst has happened earlier than expected, but I can't say I'm bothered; the house is being emptied even as we speak." Her father scowled, "No, don't be like that; this means that all the so-called 'status symbols' of my marriage have gone, and the feeling of relief is even more pleasurable than I could have expected. The inflated values he put on his possessions, as he called them, is over; he's taken the lot and apart from the pictures and the clocks, I couldn't be happier. I'm probably going back to an empty house, hopefully, with some basic furniture in it, but nothing else."

"What does the solicitor say?"

"Stay where I am, do not go home tomorrow; it's no good getting in the police as it's a domestic matter and he's entitled to take his 'possessions' regardless of my feelings, and on Monday he'll seek an injunction forbidding him entry. He's no doubt taken all he wants, and the injunction will give me permission to change the locks for security. It seems sensible to me and now I don't have to worry about the wretched things nor insure them anymore, after a while I shan't miss them, they were only inanimate objects; now if he tried to take the girls…that would be entirely different, they really are the most precious things in my life and I'll never give them up."

"Well, I hope he lives to regret his actions; you wait, the wheel will come full circle and he'll learn a hard lesson. Are you going to put the girls to bed now? If you are, I'll fill your mother in about what's happening and we'll talk when you come down. Don't worry about the school, I'll speak to the headmaster on Monday morning. I think you ought to have someone with you when you go back. I'll see if your aunt's free, she's always been fond of you and the girls and she could do with a little holiday, besides she'll see the funny side of the situation. Now come on, we'll go in and you take the girls up for their bath and bed and I'll talk to your mother."

"Thanks, Dad, its bad I know, but to me it's a blessing in disguise. I'll miss the paintings though."

"Rubbish, you can always have more later on, now come on." He strode back into the drawing-room and soon had Sophie in his arms and up onto his shoulders, touching the ceiling, "Just like your mother used to do when she was small, and no, Charlotte, I can't do you, you're too big and tall."

"Who was that on the phone?" asked her mother.

"Oh, nothing important, I'll fill you in when these little scamps have gone for their bath and bed and their old grandparents can have some peace," her father said, gently lowering Sophie to the ground.

The girls kissed their grandparents goodnight, and after many hugs went with their mother up the stairs to bed. After a while, Helen returned to the drawing-room and her parents, and the three of them talked well into the night about what to do and in particular, how to keep the girls safe. The rest of the weekend was spent with Helen's cousins, their parents, grandchildren and dogs, the grandchildren, Charlotte and Sophie disappearing happily off into the fields with the dogs. Nothing was spoken of the traumas of the previous night, it was as though nothing had happened. On Monday morning Helen's father rang the school and smoothed over the reason for the girls non-attendance. It was the first time, the headmaster had been told of the divorce and the complications connected with it. Helen was relieved that it was her father and not she herself that had confided in him; she'd been trying to summon up the courage to tell him, but she'd found it too difficult to mention the real reason for the divorce. She felt 'dirty' at the remembrance of the 'act' that she and Charlotte had heard through the bedroom door and this had tainted her reasoning and she wanted to be truthful, so she'd put off telling him.

Aunt Bea turned up for lunch and stayed and read to the children. Aunt Bea was an eccentric. Life was an adventure and whatever happened, it had to be lived and understood, nothing bothered her, everything happened for a reason; her three sons and husband had all been 'brought up' as 'engines', their bodies were 'engines' that must be fed, watered and exercised correctly otherwise they wouldn't work, and the same mandate was administered on all her great nieces and nephews as well as their parents. In her eyes a regimented and disciplined life proved beneficial to the 'engines', no matter how large or small, but always, love was there in all her actions; and now here she was happily reading to her great nieces. Sophie loved her long earrings and tried valiantly to play with them, but Aunt Bea was so animated in her portrayal of the characters in the story that they danced about all over the place, along with her hands and arms as she 'acted out' the story for Charlotte and Sophie; she was very good and her different voices fascinating to listen to, the girls were absorbed.

"Now dears, that's finished and I must go, I cannot come and stay this time, but I've made a note to come in another month with your grandparents and then I'll be interested to see what you've been up to at school. Can you wait that long?" a pause, "Of course you can. Bye dears, give me a kiss and then away with you." The girls kissed her happily and taking her by the hand, led her into the kitchen to say her 'goodbyes' to her brother and his wife. In next to no time she was in her red car, revving it hard, the gravel on the drive swirled up against the porch as the car shot like a bullet through the gates and onto the road, her brother, the girls' grandfather, cringing at the sight of the receding car waiting for the crash to happen but all was quiet as the dust settled again.

"I do wish she would be more careful when she leaves the house, we'll be picking up the pieces soon."

"Don't worry, Dad, people like her always survive despite all odds. I'm afraid we must leave too and get home before the traffic; it's been lovely being with you both and our talks have been useful. I just wish the emptying of the house hadn't occurred so soon. I'll ring you as soon as we're home and give you all the grizzly details. I'm sorry Aunt Bea isn't with us but perhaps it's just as well – there may be an awful mess to clear up and the girls may find it strange not to see familiar things. Still, the dogs will be pleased to see us all, Bill's bringing them up later today."

"I'm glad Bill's coming tonight, I'll be interested to hear what he has to say about the clearance."

"So will I."

The girls were soon in the car and the three of them turned for home and the chaos that awaited them. The journey was uneventful but as they rounded the last bend, they noticed lights on in the house. Silence fell on them all and Helen drove slowly and with terrible dread towards it. She pulled into the drive and told the girls to stay and sit tight. Slowly she got out and went up to the front door, it was open; she was greeted by the dogs and Pauline and Bill, they both kissed her.

"Sorry for the surprise," said Bill, "but we felt we had to come down and wait for you all. Jill told us what had happened but unfortunately, I was away on a case so could do nothing. It's a bit of a mess, most of the china and clocks have gone and some good furniture, and there are gaps on the walls where the pictures were; you still seem to have a modicum of furniture and most of the kitchen stuff, but I can't find any jewellery or the silver, so I suppose he's taken that."

"Oh that will have gone, but I'm not worried, he and his friend can wear it between them! The best bits are in the safe at the bank, I felt it prudent to leave everything there until the lawyers decide what's to be done with it all. I knew he'd take it, I'm only surprised he took so long but at least it's safe and he can't touch it as it's all in my name only, if you like, my insurance policy."

"Well done, but he'll want it soon enough, and I'm afraid you'll have to declare it."

"I know," Helen sighed, "I'd better get the children out of the car and into bed, school tomorrow." Helen looked with dismay at her home; she was sad to think her paintings and clocks had gone but knew the feeling would pass, she'd rebuild again soon, and with better things. Charlotte and Sophie appeared at her side and stared, "Bit bare isn't it, but at least there's no chance of breaking anything, is there?" The girls continued to stare until a dog rubbed itself against Charlotte, she fondled its ears, then spoke to Bill.

"I'm not sad it's all gone, he's welcome to it and anyway, our father's not a proper dad; he likes the company of other men."

She walked up the stairs and to her bedroom, closely followed by Sophie. Bill, Pauline and Helen stared incredulously after her, slowly comprehending what the child had said…

Helen stirred in her sleep, her brow puckered and her lips twitched, another dream was formulating, one far worse than the rest; a tragedy so etched onto her brain that no amount of distance of time would ever erase the memory of those nine horrific weeks. She moaned slightly and shifted her weight in the chair; the demon was back and in vivid technicolour.

Months passed and the awful divorce and its convoluted snakes of biting animosity continued. Helen and her lawyers had had great difficulty in persuading William to release a little extra money to buy a suitable house. He wanted her to have one miles away from the school, whereas she saw the practicality of still living nearby; the strange thing was that no owner wanted to sell to a woman on her own and with two daughters, it was amazingly old-fashioned, almost as if the Married Woman's Property Act had never existed, never been sanctioned. All the houses and people she saw were locked in a time warp. In the end, the husband of Helen's oldest friend had intervened and as if by magic, a house had been bought. It was a small end of terrace house next door to the parish church and overlooked the graveyard. A little path ran down beside the church wall and the house, safe enough for the girls to go into the town on their own, a small walled garden opened out from the kitchen and a garage was the boundary wall at the bottom. On their first night the girls had been so excited, they'd emptied the water tank having frequent baths. At last they were safe and the little estate was full of young people and other children, the girls and Helen were happy. Charlotte and Sophie earned pocket money exercising the dog of one of the residents who was out all day and picking up the shopping for an invalided lady at the end of the street. Helen was working too, and when the schools broke up, her neighbour looked after the girls.

All seemed well until they went to Yorkshire for their great grandmother's hundredth birthday. Helen had noticed that Charlotte had become listless and off her food, she'd taken her to the doctor, who'd said it was 'growing pains nothing to worry about,' but the day before they left a bruise had appeared on Charlotte's leg and the child started limping, by the evening Charlotte seemed better, the bruising diminishing, and the next day her old self. They'd driven up north in great spirits, the dogs enjoying being with the girls too and racing around the fields whenever they stopped. The greeting they all received when they arrived was huge, loads of laughter and hijinks, the aged great grandparent enjoying the fun too and tucking into the champagne that was liberally offered to her, her face wreathed in smiles of alcoholic pleasure. Her birthday celebrations went on for three days, the queen's card in pride of place on the mantelpiece in the drawing-room, it, and the recipient, having been photographed many times by the steady procession of well-wishers that came and went. The girls were now on holiday from school and they were invited to stay with their Aunt Pea (short for 'sweet pea', her nickname) for a few days whilst Helen went back to work. She had a small-holding with rabbits and goats, chickens and ducks, as well as three cats, all as fat as each other and all affectionate. Sophie couldn't wait to go, but Charlotte held back and clung to her mother. They went for a walk together, Helen all the time wondering what was wrong. Charlotte cried a lot and begged her mother to take her back with her; it took a long time for Helen to convince the child that she'd be back on Friday night to pick her and Sophie up ready for school on Monday. When they returned, Charlotte still clung to her mother; only when a small kitten was put into her hand did she release her grip and smile. Helen's aunt came up to her,

"What's wrong?"

"I don't know, I've never known her not want to stay away before, I hope she won't be a problem this week."

"Of course not, once you're gone she'll forget all about you for a few days, there's so much to do here and the boys are going to teach them both how to milk a goat. You'll see, it'll be out of sight, out of mind. Now stop worrying and have some tea before you leave. If you leave at six you'll be home by nine, just in time to settle in." Helen followed her aunt into the conservatory and saw Charlotte and Sophie sitting on the floor surrounded by kittens, happily playing with them, even the dogs were sitting quietly, occasionally sniffing a kitten or nudging it gently towards its basket.

"Come along and have a cuppa, and a piece of cake," said her aunt. "You've a long way to go and you don't want to be hungry."

Charlotte looked up anxiously, "Are you going now, Mummy?"

"Not just yet, but in a little while." She knelt down beside her daughter. "I'll be back on Friday by six, I promise, now today's Monday, so you've only three days to go before you'll be sitting up in bed on Friday morning wondering why I'm coming back as you're having such a good time." Helen watched as the little face contorted and tried to fight back the tears.

"All right, Mummy, I'll be good and see you on Friday."

"That's my darling, now let me have some tea and then come and see me off with your sister and have a cuddle."

"Do you mind if I cuddle you here, I like playing with the kittens and I'm tired, Mummy." Helen looked at her daughter and saw for the first time that the child's eyes were dark-rimmed and her skin was sallow. She drank her tea and wondered, something was definitely wrong.

"I don't mind at all, I think the kittens would appreciate your being here too."

Helen stood up and looked down at her daughter, who tried to smile back; Sophie skipped over to her mother and took her hand.

"Bye Mummy, we'll be all right and I'll look after Charlotte. I promise to be good and help. Bye."

Sophie returned to the kittens and Helen went out to the car with Aunt Pea.

"Now don't worry, Charlotte's growing up and her little body's going through all sorts of changes, she's nearly twelve and things are moving on. Now, go and have a few days off and enjoy yourself, I'm looking forward to having them here with me."

Helen climbed into her car and with a final wave headed for the motorway and the road home. Two days later the phone rang, it was her aunt.

"Helen, I think you'd better come up, Charlotte's ill and the doctor wants to see you as soon as possible. Can you get here tonight or is it a bit late?"

"I can't manage tonight but I'll leave very early tomorrow, I've got to make one or two phone calls to work etc. but if I leave by five, I can be with you by eight-thirty at the latest and we can go to the doctor's together."

"The doctor thinks she's very ill and needs to go to hospital quickly, but that nothing up here is suitable, she needs specialist care. I'll see you in time for a late breakfast," after a pause, "You're very calm, did you know she's ill?"

"Yes, I think I did, I think she's got cancer." There was a sharp intake of breath on the other end of the phone, "I've noticed a change in her over the past four weeks, and though I took her to the doctor, I wasn't entirely convinced with her diagnosis. I don't know why I said 'cancer' but I somehow knew that's what it is, as soon as you said she was ill."

"Helen, I can't believe it, there's never been any cancer in the family, ever; I hope it's not that."

"Well, we'll know tomorrow won't we, so goodbye for now and thank you for telling me." Helen put the receiver down quickly, she was shaking so much, even she wondered why she'd mentioned that dreadful word, inwardly it had shocked her. She hurriedly made her phone calls and set her alarm for four o'clock; tomorrow was going to be a very bad day.

The following morning saw her up before the alarm went off and on the road north before five. It was a beautiful morning and the dawn came quickly in a rosy glow. Helen was able to drive in comparative peace for the first hour and a half and enjoy the trip, but then the traffic became difficult, and every yard of the road seemed to be fought over to bring her nearer to her daughter, the doctor and analysis of the child's sudden illness. Helen tried to think where Charlotte had been and who she'd stayed with in the previous few weeks, but nothing presented itself; she just had to get to her and fast. Another half an hour passed in frustration and irritation at the cars on the road and their inconsiderate drivers, but just when it seemed the journey would never end, the turning to her aunt's home came into view. 'At last,' thought Helen, 'journey's end and a good cuppa!' She pulled up in front of the house as her aunt opened the door and greeted her, she looked drawn; little Sophie followed her down the steps and hugged her mother.

"You've made good time, come in and have some breakfast, I've made some flap-jacks and there are fresh eggs that Sophie gathered this morning." Helen kissed her aunt and picked up Sophie and cuddled her.

"I'm off to play with my friends, they've got a pony and I'm going to ride it today."

A Land Rover pulled into the drive and a young man and a dog got out. "I'm here to pick up a little girl who wants to ride and muck out the stable, is she here?" He looked around with mock curiosity, finally noticing Sophie. "You're clean, that'll never do…come on dog, make her dirty and more like a farm worker!" The dog duly obliged and Sophie squealed in protest as she and the dog got into the car.

"Bye Mummy, see you later, this is Ted." They all waved and had soon disappeared down the lane and out of sight.

Helen followed her aunt into the kitchen. Charlotte was dressed and sitting at the table drawing, she looked up and her mother saw for the first time how tired and listless the child was, she gently put her arms around her and felt no life in the little form, it was like holding a lifeless doll.

"Hello Mummy, I'm so glad you're here, and I'm sorry I've been a nuisance and had to go to the doctor. We've got to see him again and then you and I can go home and I'll get better."

"Quite right but let Mummy have some breakfast first, she's had a long drive."

"Do you mind?" questioned Helen.

"No, Mummy, you're here and that's all that matters, I'll get better now."

Helen and her aunt exchanged glances, and Helen leant against the Aga whilst her food was cooking, staring at the little vulnerable creature looking at her so trustingly. She smiled back at her and then talked about what she'd been doing these last two days and trying to be cheerful before they saw the doctor and learnt his prognosis. It was a difficult hour but Helen knew that for the sake of Charlotte, she had to keep calm, as if nothing were wrong. It was just another childhood ailment causing a problem now, but would be, with the right medicine, cured in a few days. Time passed and in no time the three of them were in the doctor's surgery. Charlotte knew what to do and went into the consultancy room, where the doctor examined her again, before coming back into his office and sitting down.

"Mrs Sands, how do you do?" He extended his hand across the desk and shook Helen's. "Mrs Sands, I understand you'd like to know the truth, straight, am I right?"

"Yes, I want to know everything and the treatment and how long the illness will take to cure, and, I suppose, what it is."

"Right, well, your aunt brought Charlotte in to see me because she was worried about her, she seemed tired all the time and wanted to rest. I took some blood and I've had it analysed and in my opinion your daughter is extremely ill and must be placed in hospital as soon as possible. I have the blood results here; do you know how to read a result?"

"Yes, I think I can remember, I worked in a hospital before Charlotte was born."

"Good, here it is." He handed the piece of paper over to her and she glanced at it, most was too complicated but one thing did stand out, Charlotte's white blood cell count was at fifty-five thousand, her red blood cell count negligible; she looked up at him, he was watching her steadily and waiting for her reaction. "Yes, it's very bad. In my opinion it could be one of four things, whooping cough, a virus, cancer or scarlet fever, but I think it's either cancer of the blood known as leukaemia, or a virus. I'm so sorry." He looked down at his notes, Helen asked,

"How long has she got?"

There was a sharp intake of breath from her aunt, but the doctor studied Helen carefully.

"Unless we get her into hospital straightaway, a week, possibly ten days, and even if they start to cure her, I hope she still has the strength to take the treatment."

Aunt Pea stifled her tears, the doctor handed her a tissue.

"My obvious question now is which hospital and how do I get her in?" said Helen, "I must leave as soon as possible."

"I've got all the papers here and done for you, I've made arrangements for Charlotte to be admitted to the Radcliffe tomorrow morning at nine o'clock. I'll fax these papers over to them today, but I'm also giving you an extra set to take too. I'm dreadfully sorry, I really am; you have a very long and hard road ahead of you. I also understand from your aunt that you're in the midst of a divorce, this makes the road even worse; I sincerely hope that you can manage." He extended his hand and shook Helen's firmly. "I've given Charlotte a small sedative to relax her for the journey home, if she's on the back seat, with a bit of luck, she'll sleep most of the way; drive carefully, all will be well till tomorrow. Goodbye."

He smiled and fetched Charlotte from the back room and gently put her into the back of the car. Helen turned to him again,

"Thank you for all your help, goodbye."

Helen turned to her tearful aunt, "I'll run you home and have some coffee and then be on my way. At least I can take my time, nothing to do till tomorrow but look after Charlotte. Can you cope with Sophie for the time being? Tell her I'll ring her tonight when we're back. I'd rather like to get within striking distance of the hospital as soon as possible."

"Yes, let's get back now and get you on your way. I can't believe she's so ill."

"Neither can I, but her white blood cell count is so high, she really is very ill indeed."

They returned to the farm and after an hour, Helen gently put Charlotte back into the car and made her as comfortable as possible, said her farewells to her aunt and turned the car around to face the road and the long journey ahead.

Chapter 6

Helen looked down incredulously at her daughter and the rivers of disease coursing down her leg and up into her thigh and beyond. The child was quiet, heavily sedated, and breathing deeply. There was no chance of her waking up and talking; she was so different from the hopeful girl of yesterday. Very soft wool and what looked like blown-up plastic bags had been laid around her, cushioning her against anything sharp.

"I'm sorry, Mrs Sands, but this morning one of the nurses noticed a slight mark on her leg and I'm afraid gangrene's set in. We've all been very careful how we've handled her, but as we told you yesterday, with Charlotte's red blood count only at six per cent, the slightest rough touch to her skin, by anything, cotton wool, a piece of lint, the slightest thing, would cause a lesion and a wound. I'm afraid she's now no means left to fight the cancer and now gangrene, her immune system is too weak." This to Helen was a death knell, it couldn't be true, what he'd just said had to be a worst-case scenario.

"But yesterday I was told she was in remission, and I was asked last night to come in today to see if my marrow would be a match for her. I know my blood's no good… I can't believe what I'm seeing; so what happens now?" She looked at him calmly, willing a miracle to happen, she listened quietly.

"I'm afraid we make her as comfortable as possible and when she wakes and the pain is bad, we'll give her morphine. You must understand that the pain will get steadily worse as the gangrene spreads; we can do nothing more for her but watch and wait. She *was* in remission yesterday and even last night. We only noticed the lesion this morning, it was tiny, how it happened is anyone's guess. In a normal child she'd heal easily, but as I said before, Charlotte's immune system is now non-existent."

"So, in effect, you're waiting for her to die, and an agonising death."

Helen studied the young doctor's face, it was blank. All the weeks that had passed of trying and trying again were over, this life was finished, the healthy tissue invaded by blackness and decay; yet still her heart and lungs strongly soldiered on, the organs of her body fighting for survival; but now the hideous disease was gradually beginning to party, its omnipresent contortions gradually taking control and its henchman, Death, becoming the victor. Helen's mind was full of anger that a child, *her child* could be so stricken at such an early age by Death, her fight to the death for her child's life nothing but a futile exercise. The one word that circumnavigated her muddled mind was 'why'. 'Why her? Why not me?' She looked again at the beautiful slim hand, the long nails and the gangrenous blue of the dying blood vividly illuminated against the white skin, lying peacefully on the sheet. She looked again at the doctor, his eyes tired, the sense of futility etched on his sombre face, she spoke, "Please don't let her suffer, don't let her feel the awful pain, will you?"

"No, we won't let her suffer, she'll die quite naturally, but when…I can't say. Why don't you go and get a cup of tea, we're here looking after her, you must take a break. If you like I'll get sister to come with you."

"Thank you but no, I'd rather be on my own. I'll just get a glass of water from the dispenser, I really don't want to leave her; I want to see her alive for as long as possible, even in this state. I'll have plenty of time to re-live my memories soon."

Helen felt herself starting to give way to tears, she gulped hard and went to find the water dispenser; she would on no account show any weakness, it would be too much of an imposition on the nurses to cope with her tears when they were working so hard for her daughter's welfare, and anyway, it was not how she'd been brought up. A stiff upper lip was normal in her family, not the modern way of break down and wail, and now she summoned up all her strength to adhere to the dictum. There would be plenty of time later, in the privacy of her own home for tears, now it must be 'no fuss' for as long as this final scenario took to play out its final act. There was a tap on her shoulder, and Helen turned to find her cousin standing beside her,

"I thought I'd pop down to see you and Charlotte, of course, but I hear she's taken a turn for the worse."

Helen looked at him and before she could say anything, Johnnie had put his arms around her and stood silently holding her close. Helen was so tired she could neither speak nor cry, so she allowed herself to be held, his strength and warmth seeping into her racked body. After a while she pulled away from him.

"Johnnie, I'm so glad to see you; how good of you to come and visit us both here in this…place and at this time."

"Yes, it's a bit of a hole I find you in, and I can't believe it's happening, it's like a dream. The trouble is, we already know the reality and it's definitely no dream. My mother told me Charlotte was gravely ill and that your divorce was still going on. How on earth are you coping…death and destruction around you at the same time. If you like, I'll stay with you until at least *this* terrible ordeal is over; and afterwards, keep in touch until the divorce is finished, would that be OK?"

"Thanks, Johnnie, but no thanks; I really can't cope with anyone in the house at the moment. Biddy's coming on Wednesday for the night and I'll welcome that, but anything else really is a non-starter. Until this bloody business is over, I've just got to stick it out and I'm best doing that on my own. I hope you understand; I'm going to need an awful lot of support when it's over, but at the moment I'm running on auto-pilot."

He turned and looked at his cousin, her face set into a mould of haphazard lines, all seemingly determining the road ahead, her eyes deep ringed pools of tired and faded blue.

"I understand, but just remember I'm at the end of a telephone line should you need me. There's no need to stand alone completely; now is the time to use the family in any way you can."

"I know, but I cannot explain to any of you what I want, because I don't know myself; if you like it's a terrible learning curve, this living with creeping death. You know ultimately it'll happen but when and how is the unknown factor, and that's the awful tunnel I'm in, there's no light at the end of it, just gloom and despondency. The last nine weeks have been peppered with some wonderful days, where Charlotte's responded well to treatment, to the extent that I've been able to take her home and enjoy time with her. We've gone to bed thinking about what we

70

might do the following day, but the following day's dawned and she's been in pain or nauseous, and then I've had to admit defeat and take her back to hospital and watch the relief of being there come back into her face. This is a terrible sentence I'm under, and with the divorce as well and his constant demands for custody of the girls, I'm living two lives."

"Surely, he's not making demands even now, and at this time?"

"Oh yes, he's even asked me to donate her organs, the ones that are healthy, but luckily I know I can't do that, this form of leukaemia is too rampant and there's no cure, she has the mylo-myelocytic variety; it affects just one in a hundred thousand and my daughter had to be that one. Another fifty years on into the future, and they'll probably have found a cure but not now in the seventies. I'm resigned to her dying within the next few days, she's been ill for just nine weeks."

Johnnie stayed talking until Helen was called back into the child's room; he came with her and stood staring down at the living corpse, his eyes filled with tears. Helen touched his hand. "Don't, Johnnie, please don't otherwise I'll not be able to cope." He faced her and saw the fortitude and courage in her eyes. He nodded and turned away, Helen following.

"I'm glad I've seen her, be brave as I know you will be. I'll tell mother, she'll be pleased I came." He gave Helen another hug, and she watched him disappear down the corridor to the open exit; he waved and was gone, she turned back to Charlotte's room.

The following day her parents came. As usual, Charlotte was heavily sedated and sleeping. Her mother was moist-eyed and incapable of speech; her father came around the edge of the bed and gave his daughter a kiss, she smiled back at him.

"Sorry I'm late, but I had to see the consultant, they want to come in and wake her and try her with another drug; seems a shame when she's sleeping so peacefully, but I suppose they know what they're doing."

Her father nodded, they moved to one side as the nurses and doctors came in, their feet barely gliding on the green linoleum, the instruments of medicine quietly placed on the table beside her bed. Charlotte woke of her own volition and suddenly said loudly and clearly 'The Lord's Prayer'; the whole room froze into a timeless tableaux, dumbfounded at her outburst. When she'd finished, she sank back onto her pillows, desperately fighting for breath, her eyes wildly moving across them all. Helen's parents and a nurse were asked to leave the room whilst the doctor injected her arm, this time with heroin; the doctor looked at Helen, "I'm afraid the morphine's now too mild for the pain. The gangrene has spread too far, heroin is our only option." Helen watched as the drug was slowly pushed into her daughter's arm; she realised that Charlotte's main organs were too strong, she had to be helped to die. She put her hand to her mouth and cried for the first time, the despair and hope of the past weeks washing over her; a nurse held her close. The doctor, now finished, spoke to her gently, "I cannot let her suffer, you must now prepare yourself for the end. I suggest you go home tonight and come back first thing tomorrow. I don't believe she'll go tonight, but if things do deteriorate, I'll ring you. Are your parents staying with you?"

"No, my mother won't be able to stand these final hours. To be frank, I'd rather be on my own, Charlotte is my daughter and nobody else's, I want to be alone with her today and tomorrow."

The doctor smiled and patted her arm, he called to her parents. "You can come back in now, we've finished for the moment, but I'd rather you didn't stay too long, our nursing is going to be pretty continuous now."

They came slowly back into the room, incredulous looks on both their faces as they sat down beside Helen. None of them spoke, each lost in their own thoughts and the dreadful realisation that soon a life would end, her mother tried to speak but nothing came. An hour passed and Helen got up, she spoke as cheerily as she could,

"Come on, let's get some tea and then I think you should go home. I love your being here but really there's nothing any of us can do, and the doctor's already told me to go home, and I'll do that after I've said goodbye to you both."

Her father turned to his wife and gently helped her to stand; she turned to Helen, who opened the door and guided her mother outside as the nurses came into the room. "It's for the best," said her father and the three of them went to the hospital canteen. The tea was welcoming as was the chatter around them, as for them, hardly a word was spoken.

"If you're finished, I'll walk with you both to the door and then I'll go back and sit with her for a while before going home. Come on, you both look exhausted."

Helen put her hand under her mother's arm and gently lifted her out of the chair; she and her father looked at Helen and mechanically walked towards the entrance. They turned and Helen kissed them both, "I'll ring you tomorrow, now drive carefully and go home; as I said before, neither you nor I can do anything now, I'm afraid we must wait." Helen watched until they reached the car park and then went back to her daughter. A small lamp on a table beside the bed cast a warm glow across the child's silent body, a nurse sat in the chair beside it. "If I may I'll stay for another few minutes, I find it very peaceful in here."

The nurse nodded, and Helen stood and watched her child sleeping, probably for the last time. How many times in her short life had she done this, and now, how she wished she'd stayed longer, enjoyed seeing her grow through the years.

"Mrs Sands, I'm afraid you'll have to go now, we've to change the dressings on her back and buttocks, and I can't let you see the wounds, they're rather deep and smell bad." The young nurse was standing beside her, the others creeping like spectres in behind her. They moved to the bed, and Charlotte woke and clearly saw her mother.

"What on earth are you doing here? Go home and let these nurses rest."

It was the last thing she ever said and reluctantly Helen left.

The next day was bright and sunny, Helen made Biddy's bed, left a note in the kitchen and warned her neighbours that Biddy would be arriving between four and five and asked that they let her in. After all was agreed, she set off on the weary journey back to the hospital and Charlotte. Would today be the last time she'd see her alive, she didn't know, all she knew was that she had to get to the hospital as fast as possible and to the sanctuary of Charlotte's room. She walked quickly through the hospital and the labyrinth of passages to her room, would she be alive still? Helen opened the door to be greeted by a sickly sweet smell intermingled with three vases of perfumed flowers and open windows; she knew the smell, it was the smell of decay and decomposition, in effect the child was being eaten by Death, and its breath was foul; its victim slept. Helen sat beside the bed and took the clammy hand in hers and watched as Death gorged its way through the paths of blood running down her arm, its putrefaction seeping into the nooks and crannies of her little body. She laid the hand on her lap and took out her pad and pen, she had to write to Sophie and explain. Calmly, she wrote in an easy manner, she told her she had to stay and make sure that Charlotte, like the little peas she and Sophie used to shell and eat, went to heaven and that what was left here, like the pea pods, was properly thrown away. She finished the letter by telling Sophie that she loved her very much and so did Charlotte, and that she'd see her very soon. Helen signed the letter and addressed the envelope, whilst doing this, Charlotte's hand slipped off her mother's knee. Though she was still breathing, Helen knew she'd gone. She stayed for a few moments in the precious privacy of the room with her daughter and her thoughts before bending down and kissing the still warm face and smoothing the few remnants of hair surrounding it. Reluctantly, reality came back, and she then went to find the nurse; for the first time in nine weeks she suddenly felt buoyant, Charlotte was at last, at peace.

"Why Mrs Sands, you look different."

"Do I? How strange, Charlotte's still breathing but to me, she's gone. I've just been writing to her sister and such a strange feeling of 'relief' came over me after I finished the letter. I'm going home now, I don't believe there's any point in my being here tonight. I'll see you tomorrow."

Helen left the hospital and slowly returned home and to Biddy. Later that night after they'd eaten, she went out into the garden and listened to a blackbird singing its evening hymn; 'The same song as the morning Charlotte was born,' thought Helen. The phone rang, Biddy picked it up and brought it out to Helen and waited.

"Mrs Sands, Charlotte died five minutes ago, I'm very sorry."

"I know, a blackbird told me just as it did at her birth, it's been singing its heart out for the last ten minutes in the apple tree here in the garden. Thank you for all you've done for me over the last nine weeks; it's been a terrible journey but now it's over and at last, you can get some rest. Please thank everyone and I'll be in in the morning. One last favour, please will you dress her in the clean nightie I brought with me today, Sister knows where it is, and could you place her bear, little Fonz, in her hand?"

"I'll do all that and look forward to seeing you in the morning. Good night, enjoy your blackbird, I've heard of this happening before." The phone went dead, a chapter of Helen's life was over forever, now the grieving would begin and the trauma of recovery start. Biddy turned to Helen and gave her a glass of wine, they stood together in the little garden and the gathering dusk. Helen said, "You know, I once asked her if she was frightened at all, her reply was 'No, why should I be, they're trying to help.' She had so much courage, I don't think I'd be able to cope given the same situation."

Biddy looked at her cousin and linked her arm with Helen's, they raised their glasses and stood listening to the blackbird's final hymn.

Chapter 7

She lent on the railings looking out to sea and at the people and their children milling around her and on the beach below. In the crowd she thought she saw the face of a young girl she recognized, automatically she put up her hand and waved calling out the girl's name, 'Charlotte'. She felt the reassuring touch of her father's hand on her shoulder.

"It's all right, love, it's not her just someone else."

She turned and faced him, her eyes and unsaid words mirroring all she'd been through during the last nine weeks; horror, frustration, hope, futility, realisation and finally despair that nothing could be done; the child she'd borne just eleven and a half years earlier had gone; cancer, the great leveller, had brought its cruelty to a young life on the threshold of adulthood. A young brain eager to be filled with knowledge, a mind of untapped intelligence and a face of developing beauty.

"But it's so like her, I've made a fool of myself again, sorry. I wonder how long it'll be before I stop 'seeing' her. I miss her so much, she was a real strength to me during the awful divorce from William, now I've nothing, no 'prop'. Sophie's great but still too young to understand."

"No, you've not made a fool of yourself, those people will just think you're eccentric or ill." He smiled at his daughter before continuing, "It'll take you a long time to get over her death, perhaps you never will, for the time being try and accept what's happened to you. The worst of it is that none of us knows what you're going through and we all feel so helpless; this is a frightful battle that only you can win with time. Why don't you take yourself away, just on your own, for a while, somewhere far away from here."

Helen looked at her father, his eyes too, showed the strain of the past weeks; her mother had taken everything so badly that one began to wonder if it was she, and not Helen, who'd lost a daughter.

"Thanks for that, actually, I was going to tell you all tonight that I've booked to go to Greece on a four-day package, it's what I can safely afford. I was hoping that Sophie could continue her schooling up here until the end of term."

"I see no reason why not, it's a good idea, but why go to Greece?"

"I want the warmth and the sea, I thought the sea and a strange place would assuage grief more easily; also, whilst I'm there, I could pretend to be a different me and not what I've become these last weeks. I've got to be strong for Sophie, and I'm not at the moment. My flight's booked for Thursday and I come back the following Tuesday morning."

"I'll give you the money for your break, and we'll look after Sophie. I think it a good idea to keep her at the little school here, just until the end of term, but then you'll have to take her back. Let's have a talk at Christmas about her future education. She's a good little thing, and I think she'll have settled down more by then; anyway, I'm very fond of that little 'scamp'. I'll take you to the airport and pick you up again next Tuesday. In the meantime, not a word, I'll find a reason why you're not going to be here."

"That's all right, I've already told Sophie I've got some interviews this weekend and she's accepted my explanation. I know it's a bit of a lie, but it seemed easier to do it this way as she won't ask many questions."

"I see your point, but I hate lying and especially to one as young as Sophie, just don't do it again, at the moment she's too vulnerable. Come on let's find the others and get an ice cream."

The last few days flew by and she left for the airport and Greece alone, her father not taking her, this time she needed to be alone. The little hotel was quiet and a path led down to the quay, where the brightly coloured fishing boats bobbed up and down like so many exotic birds and fishermen chatted away to each other whilst mending nets and re-painting their boats ready for the next fishing trip. They called out to her and she waved back, none of them spoke English and she knew no Greek, but somehow they all knew what was meant. One of them, a young dark-haired man, asked by signs if she'd like to help mend a net, she agreed and was soon sitting amongst them listening to their chatter and copying what they were doing and for the first time laughing at her efforts, she was content for the first time in weeks. Two hours passed and a round and jolly woman wearing a brightly coloured scarf appeared, calling to them all, she had a large basket lined with gingham containing a carafe of wine, bread, cheese and smoked fish. The men dropped what they were doing and greeted her fulsomely, immediately relieving her of the basket and gesticulating wildly, laughing uproariously. The woman turned to the man nearest to her and muttered, they exchanged words obviously directed at Helen, then she eyed her up and down; she smiled a toothless grin and said "ENGLISH" in a loud voice as though Helen were deaf, a lined and bronzed hand was extended to Helen, who took it in both of hers, "Yes," she said and smiled warmly. The old woman gestured to Helen to sit and covered her skirt in a snowy white napkin and indicated the food. Helen ate and felt the warmth of the wine revive her. The kindness of these simple uncomplicated people filled her poor and battered soul with peace and joy.

By degrees, the hotel staff and the fishermen realised that Helen was different from the usual tourist; she'd been hurt and had come to their island to be healed. It seemed to them that the solution to her troubles, whatever they might be, was easy. Their simplistic solution was to care for her and make her smile, so they filled her days with understanding and joy, taking her to rocky coastlines and grottoes and showing her how to fish 'their way', and soon Helen forgot why she was there, she was so wrapped up in the kindness of these people. Too soon the little holiday was at an end; on the last night she asked the hotel if they would lay on food and wine for them as her way of saying 'thank you' to them all for their generosity, they agreed and in no time the little quay was decorated with fairy lights and tables groaning with food and wine and filled with laughter and dancing. Helen was swept up into the arms of the handsome fisherman and his friends and taught how to dance the Greek way. She revelled in it all but all too soon it was over; they had work to do the following day but would see her off to the mainland and home, realisation returned to Helen and she cried silently to herself.

Helen left the hotel the following morning, her idyll at an end, tears stinging the backs of her eyes. As she reached the boat for the mainland and home, singing greeted her and a basket of presents was put on the seat beside her, she turned and waved until the little quay was out of sight. Normality returned and now, with no more pretence, the past horrors of a death and its aftermath loomed large on her horizon.

The journey back to England was uneventful, the plane being full of disgruntled holidaymakers, sad to be leaving the warmth, blue sea and white houses of Greece. Helen was thankful that no one spoke to her so she had time to remember her break and to formulate her plans for the coming months. She drove her little car into her parents' drive and parked in front of the front door, her father was already on the step waiting to greet her.

"Glad to have you back, you look well, the rest has done you good. Mother's in the kitchen; I'll take your bag up to your room and then I suggest you go up soon and change. Your clothes are a little too 'summery' and Sophie will be suspicious!"

Helen kissed her father and went into the house to see her mother. "Hello Mum, it's me I'm back," she said cheerily.

"Oh, how well you look, I'm so glad to have you back. I'll put the kettle on whilst you go up and change before Sophie gets back. She's home early today." Helen kissed her mother and went upstairs, the warmth of the family love enveloping her. She tried not to dwell too long in silence in her room and quickly changed and unpacked the little presents she'd bought for them all and re-joined them downstairs.

"I've brought you each a present, it's nothing special, just locally made craft things. The people were so kind and life was simple, I actually enjoyed myself, and managed to forget for a short time and stop thinking of Charlotte. Sounds bad to say that, I know, she'd have loved the island, it was so warm and inviting... I'll never forget her, you know that, but for a short time I did. I wonder how the dogs will react when Sophie and I get home, it was good of Bill to take them in. Actually, I'm looking forward to seeing the little house, I'll repaint Sophie's room and put in some new bits for her, but I intend to leave Charlotte's room exactly as it was for the time being. Will you be coming to stay at Christmas or do you want us here? If you come to me, then I'll have to rearrange Charlotte's room or you can go in mine, whatever you decide will be fine with me." Helen suddenly stopped talking and realised she'd monopolised the conversation. "Sorry, I'm rabbiting, sorry."

Her father patted her hand, "It's all right, you carry on. Look, here's Sophie, getting out of Jean's car. Go and say hello. Jean's brought Sophie home each day and seems such a nice young woman, and has been so helpful where Sophie's concerned, nothing's been too much trouble; your mother and I have really appreciated her being around. By the way, Sophie adores her son."

Her father opened the front door and was immediately hugged by Sophie, who then saw her mother and stopped hugging her grandfather; she turned and looked at her mother and said solemnly,

"Charlotte's not coming back, is she, Mummy? She's gone now, hasn't she?" Helen was taken aback at the child's brazen statement, but before she could answer, Sophie continued, "Grandma and Grandpa have looked after me and so has Auntie Jean and this is her son Tommy, we're in the same class together. Say hello to Mummy, Tommy." Sophie went and stood holding her mother's hand as Tommy looked at Helen, and said in a very serious voice,

"How do you do, Mrs Sands? I'm very pleased to meet you, I like Sophie very much." Tommy extended his hand and carefully shook Helen's.

"I'm delighted to meet you too, Tommy, perhaps you'll come and play and have tea with us one day soon."

"I'd like that very much." He and Sophie went off to the kitchen in search of Sophie's grandmother. Helen turned to Jean, she was very pretty and slim, with smiling eyes and a wide, honest face. She smiled at Helen,

"Hello, I'm sorry about your loss, if I can help with Sophie in any way, please ask. It may be too soon to ask but I will anyway, why don't you come and have a meal with us? I'm afraid it's a bit chaotic at home as my husband enjoys rescuing animal waifs and strays, usually injured and found on the road or in the woods. I'm afraid he's like that, can't bear to see anything hurt. Sophie and Tommy love taking care of them, so what about it? By the way, I'm Jean."

Helen looked at Jean seeing nothing but fun, compassion and kindness in her face, "And I'm Helen, but you probably know that already. I'd love to come; I really would. Thank you so much for asking us, Jean."

"Good, why don't you come over for lunch on Saturday at twelve? Just bring yourselves and boots, the woods are bound to be wet, we can go for a ramble on the downs the other side of the woods; it's a lovely walk, not too tiring, and you and I can talk and get to know each other a bit."

Jean called, "Goodbye, I'm going now," in the direction of the kitchen, and Thomas and Sophie emerged, their mouths stuffed with cake.

Sophie followed Tommy to the car and then ran back to her mother, catching hold of her hand tightly. "See you Saturday, bye." Jean waved and was gone; Helen turned and faced her mother, Sophie still clung to her.

"We've had an invitation for lunch on Saturday, do you mind if Sophie and I go to Jean's?"

"No, delighted; your father and I have a lot of gardening to catch up with, so we'll be busy all day, no, go and enjoy yourself and make new friends." She looked down at Sophie still clinging to her mother's hand, "I'm afraid you've now a 'little shadow'; she'll cling for a long time, my dear."

"I know, and I can think of nothing nicer." She picked up her daughter and tickled her, the child giggled, Helen loved the sound. "I've something for you to try on but only after you've had a bath and washed your dirty, sticky face." The child wriggled out of her mother's arms and went to find her grandfather. Helen looked at Sophie and then her mother, her mindset changed. "You know, I've just had another thought; why don't I just stay with Sophie here in the north? I really don't want to go south just yet, and I think Sophie will be happier up here at school with her new friends for the next six months to a year; just until Charlotte's death is a distant memory to her, which it will be after a time. I'll have to go back and get the dogs and make sure I can let the house for a while, but there's no reason why I can't rent something up here near to you both and find a job, would you mind?"

Her mother beamed, "Your father will be so pleased, we were hoping you'd decide to stay near us for a while, just until the dust settles and Sophie feels a little happier; who knows, you might decide to stay here altogether."

"Who knows indeed, but I think I must be practical and not think too far ahead." Helen paused before her grieving memories suddenly returned like a flood. "You've no idea what it's like, this grieving business, I wake up sometimes thinking I've heard her call out in pain, just like she sometimes did in the last few days at home; more often than not though, she'd just lay there, still, in the dark, not moving or making a sound, not wanting to disturb me. I wonder what she thought about in those terrible dark hours, she must have felt so alone, I hope 'something', unknown to us, was there for her. That's the trouble with cancer, it's creeping viciousness is so terrible, no one can describe what it must feel like to an individual suffering with it, we can only watch and imagine, but to a child, my child, the fear she felt must have been awful, that's why I hope that there was 'something' in her wakeful moments to comfort her." The horror of those nine weeks suddenly overcame her and her eyes filled with tears, she turned to her mother, pain etched on her face, "I wish she'd called out, I would have preferred to have sat with her and held her close..." She paused before continuing and startling her mother with her revelations. "You know her spleen enlarged...when she tried to get up to go to the bathroom or downstairs, the pain was so intense, she'd lie back on the pillows, her little face ashen and pant heavily until it passed...but, she never cried out...I'll never forget her eyes in those moments, wide and terrified, looking at me for comfort, and I couldn't give it, I was helpless, impotent. The enormity and complexities of the disease too great to understand, and the cruelties of the medicines given to her to combat it too awful to watch...and my child bore it all with an inner strength which came from God knows where, for all that time."

Helen swallowed hard, reliving the memory and her own fear at the time, she breathed in and continued, "When Sophie was up here with you all, Charlotte and I would sit on the sofa together, her head on my shoulder, reading; she loved the 'Wind in the Willows' and loved reading aloud, which she did so well, her favourite chapter was 'The Piper at the gates of Dawn', do you remember it...? The one about the little otter that got lost and was found safely sleeping, at the feet of the little satyr. I loved those moments and those final days with her at home, I never wanted anything or anyone to come and interfere, it was so peaceful… Old Dr Murphy did call and she enjoyed that and so did I, he was full of stories and jokes and made her laugh… Do you know I can still hear that laugh…and her voice sometimes, it's comforting. I find myself having the odd conversation with her; she always knew the right answer to any problem when she was alive and now, it seems, she's continuing to advise me from beyond the grave."

Her mother stared at her daughter, unable to comprehend the horrors she'd been through nor the traumas of recovery to come. She hung her head in sorrow and touched her daughter's arm before returning to the sanctuary of her kitchen. Helen watched her go, 'Poor Mum,' she thought, 'she really can't cope.' She turned and went upstairs to Sophie and her bath.

Sophie greeted her mother with too many bubbles in the bath and a lot on her face and hair. "I thought I'd help, but I think I've made too many bubbles." Her little eyes were like saucers as she searched her mother's face for probable disapproval, but there was none, instead Helen bent down to the little girl and gave her a hug before continuing to bath her and play games with the bubbles. She looked at Sophie, it seemed to her that the little girl had suddenly grown up, gone was the mischievous grin and 'devil may care' attitude of a few months ago; here was a child now fearful of life and what lay ahead. Helen realised she must act very soon and make Sophie's life a happy one again; the decisions about where to live and what to do suddenly became clear.

"Would you like to stay up here at school with your new friends for a little while longer, and shall we find a little cottage to live in so they and Grandpa and Grandma can come and visit us?"

Sophie's face lit up, "Yes please, I'd love that, but what about our old house, what'll we do with that and the dogs?"

"I thought I'd let it for a while, just until next spring, and then when we want to we'll go back and visit it, what do you think? I'll have to go back very soon and get in touch with the agents and make sure it's neat and tidy, ready for letting; and I'll pick up the dogs at the same time and bring them back; what do you think of that idea?"

"I think it's a great idea, so long as nothing of Charlotte's is touched. Perhaps we can put things in the attic and have a 'mini Harrods', just like Grandma and Grandpa have."

Helen laughed, "I don't think we've as much to put in the attic as they've got, but I like the idea, well done you for thinking of it, and yes, it'll be good to have the dogs up here with us." She hugged the sweet-smelling child and carried her into the bedroom. "Heavens, you're a lump, what have you been eating? Now come and see what I've brought back for you and let's see if it fits."

Sophie scrambled onto her bed, Helen sighed remembering how carefully the parcel had been wrapped as she watched the child tear the wrapping paper to shreds, anxious to get at the contents. The pretty dress that had been hand-embroidered by the fisherman's mother tumbled out onto the bed, suddenly the sweet aroma of the little Greek island filled the room and the warmth of the people enveloped Helen again. The dress was a beautiful sky blue and the skirt was covered in little pink and white posies and butterflies, Sophie held it up to her and danced around the room, making it float and reveal the dainty petticoats underneath, Helen slipped it over her daughter's head and watched as it perfectly cascaded over the child's pyjamas underneath, "Can I go and show them please, Mummy?"

"Of course you can, but be careful, I don't want it marked." As she picked up the rubbish of paper and ribbon tape, she listened to the exclamations of delight from below and waited for her daughter to come running back upstairs.

"They love it, please take it off now, Mummy, and hang it up. Thank you for my present, can I wear it on Saturday and show Tommy, please?" Sophie hugged her mother and got into bed.

"I don't think so, but you can take it with you and show them, but we'll need jeans and boots to wear for Saturday, your dress would get dirty." After more chatter about the dress and when she'd wear it, Helen was finally released and a happy child went to sleep.

Her father greeted her with a glass of wine and together they went into the drawing-room to talk. The evening soon passed and plans were made for the morrow and decisions taken. Helen decided to try and see if there were any book-keeping jobs going in the town, she thought she'd start modestly in the hopes that the office she chose would realise her qualifications over time. She felt she needed 'breaking in' after having been at home for the past weeks and some of her confidence had been knocked. She wanted to see too, if she found a job, how 'they' worked before putting her stamp on any firm that employed her. It was decided she'd concentrate on her job first before finding a cottage, and that her house in the south should be rented out as soon as possible; priorities having been put in place, the three of them drank a toast in celebration and looked forward to the adventure ahead.

The following morning, after Sophie had gone to school, Helen and her father went into the little town to find suitable firms that might employ Helen. The town was quaint, it had all the usual shops and a couple of interesting pubs and the large grand old house that dominated the square. This was now divided into two, one side solicitors, the other accountants, clustered around a large market square that was transformed from parking spaces around the war memorial to a market on Wednesdays and Saturdays. Two artisan shops completed the picture, one a bakery and the other local cheeses. The smell that greeted Helen and her father from the bakery was too good and they both went in to buy 'something' for tea! Their purchases bought, Helen suggested going across to the Red Lion for a coffee, her reasoning being that 'gossip in pubs' always revealed 'something'. Unfortunately, nothing happened, so Helen decided to leave her father to see the solicitor he knew about renting a cottage for her, whilst she went into the accountants to leave her CV.

A wonderfully tall stick-thin woman with pince-nez on the end of her nose took her CV. and with animation, waved her to a seat and told her to wait, she did. After a while a door at the far end of the hallway opened and a frail old man leaning heavily on the arm of the stick thin woman emerged into the hall and stood in front of Helen.

"This is our Mr Oakham, he'd like to speak with you." It was obvious from the hand gestures of the stick-thin woman that Mr Oakham, though in charge, was also very deaf and relied heavily on her to interpret conversations, he looked up, "This is Mrs

Sands, whom I told you about a moment ago," she said very clearly and loudly.

Mr Oakham grunted, "Oh yes, yes, very nice, Mrs Trot, yes very nice indeed, she'll do." He looked Helen up and down, then taking Mrs Trot's arm again, for that was the 'stick-thin' woman's name, retraced his steps back to his den at the end of the corridor. Helen stood and watched them go, after five minutes had elapsed and Mrs Trot had not emerged, she wondered if she should go, she gathered her things together and started to edge slowly towards the front door, when a voice called to her from Mr Oakham's lair.

"Wait, one moment, Mrs Sands, I've not finished talking to you; our Mr Oakham has to be settled first before we can resume talking about your position and terms; please follow me, this way." With that Mrs Trot strode off up the stairs and into a large and airy office that was covered in papers and smelt musty. At the far end of the room there was a fireplace with a small electric fire in the aperture, an old desk and huge armchair behind it. The desk had a large brass lamp, an old-fashioned blotter and pen rack with ink wells on top, a large and ornate rug covered the floor under the desk and in front of the fire. Mrs Trot opened the window and fresh air flowed around the room, gently lifting the dust from the old files strewn about the room and allowing the particles to settle on different files and resume their unspoken audits.

"This was our Mr Oakham's room until he could no longer climb the stairs, but now it will be yours, please treat it with respect. We would like you to come in for a probationary period of one month and for that time will pay you a lesser salary than you will get should you be suitable, I hope that is satisfactory to you? Our hours are nine till five, with one hour for lunch and fifteen minutes in the morning for coffee and thirty minutes in the afternoon for tea, which is always taken in Mr Oakham's room. On Tuesday nights we have a company meeting after work to discuss any files that may be difficult and for any suggestions to be made, this means that on Wednesday mornings we start at ten. Do you have any questions?"

"No, it all seems very clear."

"Good, we'd like you to start on Friday of this week, just to settle in. I suggest you come in at ten then at coffee I can introduce you to the rest of the staff, by then I'll know what our Mr Oakham will wish to pay you. You will do some light book-keeping on Friday and we'll progress further from there, but not until your probationary period has been served. Your CV seems very good, we shall see how you progress. Come."

Mrs Trot closed the window and ushered Helen to the door and locked it behind her; descending the stairs at a canter, she stood waiting for Helen at the front door.

"May I ask, Mrs Trot, why you've employed me so quickly?"

"We need an extra pair of hands; our Mr Oakham is frail and cannot work as he used to do. He's mindful of his infirmity, but…we don't talk about it. Goodbye, Mrs Sands." She opened the door to let Helen out, the rhythm of her movement and immediate closure causing the least amount of draught in the hallway before Helen could say goodbye herself.

'Well,' said Helen to herself and immediately burst out laughing, just as her father emerged from the solicitors.

"How did you get on?" His giggling daughter took him by the arm quickly down the steps and across to the Red Lion.

"Well," said Helen again this time out loud, "I've got a job and I start on Friday at ten, but the woman who supposedly interviewed me was a real character, straight out of a Dickens story, unbelievable. I'm on probation for a month at a reduced salary and my office is like something from 'Great Expectations', very musty and full of old files but I like it, it'll be fun." Helen continued to giggle until they'd both settled down with a drink. "I can't believe what I've just experienced, its archaic, how can they ever do anything, let alone present audits correctly, for the tax-man and their clients, it's unbelievable! We're in the late seventies and yet their behaviour is pre-war. I'll be really surprised if I last long." She took a long draft of shandy and settled back in her seat, her father watching her and musing to himself.

"Well, it's better than not having anything at all, so why not make the best of a bad job for the time being? You never know, you might enjoy yourself."

"That'd be something, how did you get on about a cottage for Sophie and I, anything about?"

"Strangely enough, yes! Mr Grange has a client with a farm out on the moors behind the reservoir. His name is Bob Deanthwaite, his wife's called Jenny and their tenant has recently left and the cottage is now free. The Deanthwaites are having renovations and repainting done at the moment, but it could be ready within the month. The Deanthwaites are clients of Oakham's too, you never know, you might get to do his books!"

"I doubt it, but I'd love to go and see the cottage, do you think you could arrange it, please?"

"I'll see what I can do." Her father left the pub and went back across the square to the solicitor's. Helen continued with her drink and was aware of a tall blond-haired man coming towards her.

"I hope I'm not intruding on your thoughts, but haven't we met before? I seem to remember an upturned bag and forgotten car keys. I do hope they're not lost again." His eyes twinkled as he extended his hand to her, "My name is James Dyer."

"Yes, I vaguely remember, sometime last May, I believe. I'd had rather difficult meetings that day and you were in the window, like me, of a café that had seen better times."

"That's it, and now here you are again in this delightful old market town at least two hundred miles from where we last met. What are you doing here?"

Unease crept into Helen's mind; she did not like being accosted by 'almost' total strangers in a strange town and was certainly not interested in talking to him.

"I'm actually staying with my parents and am waiting for my father to return from the solicitor's offices, we have much to discuss together," Helen replied frostily, "Then, when we've finished our drinks, I've a daughter to collect from school." 'Hopefully,' she thought, 'these facts might put him off, usually any mention of children was a 'turn off' with people like him!' At that moment her father returned, was about to speak but restrained himself when he saw the man with Helen.

"Ah, here's my father. Dad, this is Mr James Dyer, he's just leaving; we met by chance some time ago back in Buckingham. Strange world isn't it, and, after this meeting, certainly not very big!" she stood up and smiled quizzically at the young man, who turned and said good morning to her father and left.

"That was a bit rude, dear; you never gave me a chance to respond. Did you say James Dyer? He's a respected land-owner and farmer around here, does an enormous amount for the community. His family's been in these parts for centuries. I wouldn't fall out with him if I were you, particularly as you'll be working for his accountants, and old Deanthwaite's land is next to his."

"Well, there's a surprise. I never realised you were a sycophant." She smiled sarcastically at her father, who glowered back. "I'm sorry, but if I'd been properly introduced instead of 'picked up', my behaviour would have been different; I don't like people imposing themselves on me, never have. Besides, I'm not into 'men' at the moment. How did you get on?"

"Very well, he's going to ring Deanthwaite tonight and see what he can do, we'll hear in the morning. It's not very big, just two bedrooms and the bathroom's downstairs, along with a kitchen and two separate living-rooms, so you'll get your piano in but everything else will be rather cramped. I said you wouldn't mind. Oh, it's got an inglenook, I knew you'd like that."

"Sounds perfect, I'm looking forward to seeing it, and Sophie will be over the moon. A month isn't long to wait either and I'll have plenty of time to go south and see to the house and get it let, and see the school at the same time. I'm hoping that Mr Howden, the headmaster, will keep Sophie's place open for a little while but I expect she'll have to leave, which'll be a shame as it's got a good reputation."

"You'd better make up your mind about that and quickly, I doubt whether they'll keep it after the end of next term. Come on, let's go home and talk to your mother."

"There's one other thing, Sophie and I will have to stay with you for the next month, will you mind?

"I doubt it, we've had Sophie with us for a while, a little while longer isn't going to make any difference."

Helen and her father left the pub and went across the square to the car and home. Helen noticed James Dyer talking to another man on the far side of the square, he waved and Helen's father waved back. When they got home, there was a strange car in the drive, actually it was a jeep.

"Whose is this, the logs for the winter aren't due yet, surely," muttered her father, they got out of the car and went inside, to be greeted by laughter coming from the kitchen.

"I'm glad you're back, this is Mr Deanthwaite, he says you've been asking about a cottage to rent; is this true, Helen?"

"Yes it is, actually Dad went to see the solicitor and he told us about it. How nice to meet you."

"It won't be posh, not like what you're used to, but it's clean and newly painted and it'll be just right for you an' the little maid, why don't you cum an' have a look at it? I know you've been through more than any lass should have had to face recently, your mother's bin tellin' me all about it, tragic, tragic, no other word to describe it, so what about it? I'll have to charge you somat' but not much if you decide to take it, just until you get on your feet. Could you manage fifty pounds a month, do you think, which'll include rates and water?"

"Certainly I could manage that, Mr Deanthwaite, and I'd love to see the cottage; may I come over on Saturday morning at about eleven o'clock and bring Sophie, please?"

Mr Deanthwaite's face beamed and he shook Helen's hand vigorously, "Aye, that'll be grand, lass, grand; Mrs Deanthwaite'll be right chuffed to meet you both." He stood up and with a brusque goodbye continued before leaving, "Well, I must go now, I've got cows to milk and I can't have them in a pickle." He turned, thanked them all again and doffing his cap, left the house.

Saturday couldn't come quickly enough for Helen and Sophie; Friday had been an experience for Helen at Oakham's, which she'd never forget, they were all very kind, but everything was so 'old-fashioned' in its disciplined form and yet the day's work was achieved, and in time; however, her mind was too focused on the following day and the cottage viewing to make working hard a priority, but Monday would be another day and much more concentrated.

When Helen and Sophie reached the farm, Mr Deanthwaite was waiting for them both, he was grinning from ear to ear and kindness itself in his greeting of them both.

"Champion, champion, you found us! Well, come along now, but I warn you, it won't be posh, not like what you're used to, but it's clean and newly painted and I think, will be just right for you and the little maid. Come along now, this way."

He led them across the yard and around the back of the hay store, to a white-washed cottage with a blue front door. Three windows were across the top and two on either side of the front door, a chimney at either end of the roof. Geraniums had been put in pots on either side of the front door and were manfully standing up to the weather. Helen could see gingham curtains at the windows on the top floor and heavier ones below. Mr Deanthwaite opened the front door and led them inside. The room was cosy and very quaint, full of charm and old-fashioned brown furniture; to the right of the front door was a large inglenook fireplace, the lintel decorated with horse brasses and the hearth filled with copper kettles and coal buckets. A large turkey rug lay in front of the fire and Meg, Mr Deanthwaite's collie, lay on it. Sophie immediately went over to her and the dog licked her hand. 'She's settled,' thought Helen, 'that's a relief.' To the left of the front door was another door, which led into a blue and white kitchen, a small Aga stood opposite the door and a small table and chairs in the middle of the room. Brightly coloured plates were arranged on the dresser, and a vase of wild flowers stood on the table. The two bedrooms upstairs were equally inviting, with sheepskin rugs beside the beds and large thick eiderdowns on them and pink and white curtains at the windows beside the old fitted cupboards, everywhere was spotless. Helen followed Mr Deanthwaite outside to the barn, where the farm machinery was kept and she could keep her car. At the back of the cottage was a pretty walled garden that led out from the kitchen.

"Well, lass, what do you think, is it for you or not? Yon little maid's taken with the place and my Meg, I can see meself losing 'er, she's right taken with your daughter. Any road, don't decide yet until I've shown you rest of farm, we won't be long. Come along this way."

They all followed him out of the cottage, Mr Deanthwaite was kindness itself and took Sophie's hand and pointed out the rest of the farm to them both. Sophie loved the animals and wanted to touch them all, but the farmer told her to follow him into the barn and have a look for 'something' in the straw. Sophie crept in behind him closely, followed by Meg, who disappeared behind the straw bales; suddenly there were tiny yelps and noises of greeting from behind them, and there was Meg closely followed by six little puppies. Sophie's face was a picture, and Helen thought she'd burst with excitement as she clasped her little hands together. Mr Deanthwaite picked up one of the puppies and put it into Sophie's hands,

"Be careful, lass, they're not very old and Meg's watching how you handle them. Collies are very protective and are very wary of people touching their offspring." He needn't have worried, Sophie was in her element and nothing was going to harm Meg's puppies whilst she was there. "You can help me feed them, and Meg before we go and find Mrs Deanthwaite and have some coffee, she'll have made a cake, too; now come with me, lass."

Helen watched as Sophie carefully put down the bowls for the puppies and another larger one for Meg under the guidance of Mr Deanthwaite; she watched them both and thought of Charlotte and how much she'd have appreciated the farm, the hills surrounding it, and the distant sea and coast on the horizon. A sudden feeling of enormous sadness overcame her and she turned her face towards the outside and the wind so they'd not see her moistening eyes. Soon they left Meg and her family guzzling hard and went into the farmhouse. A wonderful smell of fresh baking greeted them all and Helen's spirits lifted. The table was covered in pies and bread and homemade cakes and Mr Deanthwaite's wife was just emptying a tray of shortbread onto a plate.

"Well, here we are, Jenny, we've seen the cottage and are all in need of a drink and a homemade 'something', aren't we, lass?" He bent down to Sophie, "And we've fed Meg and the puppies."

Jenny Deanthwaite came and shook Helen's hand and bent down and ruffled Sophie's hair. "It's all ready now come and sit near the fire, everyone's always cold at first in a strange place."

The food and coffee were delicious, Helen found herself relaxing in the friendly ambience of the farmhouse and the Deanthwaites and watched as Sophie chatted away with them both, completely at home. 'Yes,' she thought, 'we could be very happy here for a while.' After coffee Helen and Mr Deanthwaite went into his study, Helen happy to talk business with him and sign an agreement, she mentioned the little dachshunds to him before signing, his only comment being 'so long as they never went near the animals and were kept on a lead within the farm, he'd not object'. He told Helen where the best 'runs' were for them well away from livestock and looked forward to seeing them after they'd moved in. They returned to the bright kitchen and found Sophie busy drying dishes and chattering away to her hostess.

"Mummy, can we stay, please? I love the cottage and I'll keep my room tidy and help too. Can I feed the puppies too, please?"

Helen hugged her daughter. "Yes, you can stay here, I've just agreed everything with M. Deanthwaite, so today we'll tell Tommy when we see him where we're going to be, and tonight, Grandma and Grandpa, they'll be so pleased that we'll be near them all." Sophie proceeded to thank the Deanthwaites but had difficulty saying their name but with great concentration she managed.

"Now one thing before you go; our name's a difficult one, so from now on I'm 'Bob' and my wife's 'Jenny', so no more Mr and Mrs Deanthwaite, I'll think I've done some'at wrong and that'll never do."

They all laughed, and Bob and Jenny walked with them to the car, Bob helped Sophie into her seat whilst Jenny put a small bag on the back seat for Sophie, saying, "That's for you and your friend Tommy later on!"

Bob turned to Sophie and said, "You never know little lass, there might be some'at waiting for you next time you come." He stroked his nose in a conspiratorial way and winked at her. Sophie's eyes were the size of saucers as she turned to wave to them both as they left the farmyard and turned for Tommy's house.

"Mummy, did you hear that, what do you think he meant, 'some' at waiting', what does it mean?"

"I haven't a clue, but I do know that Mrs Deanthwaite likes making things for village fetes, so I expect it'll be something like that for your bedroom."

Helen tried to be nonchalant, she had an idea that it'd be another dog and wondered how the two dachshunds would cope, she sighed. She continued to drive to Jean's house, all the time listening to Sophie's questions and endless chatter and thinking for the first time that now there was 'purpose and a way forward' in their lives.

Helen stirred in her sleep, a happy smile across her face. That time at the farm had been a happy one, nothing but happy memories and she and her daughter had blossomed and healed; Sophie growing into a very attractive girl with many boyfriends and she, Helen, enjoying her work and also being 'needed' on occasion! Sophie had decided for them both, to stay in the north. The school and college Sophie attended were good and suited her well. She'd learnt to ride and was a natural; this had opened many doors for her and the various balls she went too soon produced an introduction to her husband, Ian, a local farmer. Helen sighed, 'The rest as they say is history.' She slumbered on.

Chapter 8

Helen sat in the window watching last year's leaves swirling in the gathering dusk across the square. The late sun glinted on the windows, turning them to a deep yellow and warming the bricks to a rich red russet. Birds joined in the fun of the chattering leaves and swooped low across the street and catching an eddy rose again into the sky, the colours of their feathers caught in the sunlight. Nothing else was about in the square, but then nothing was ever there when she came in for tea.

Last summer it had been different – full of bustle and tourists and the cries of the vendors from the different stalls of gaudy colours, an annual tradition carried on from medieval times, but not now, it was October and all the indolent days of heat and passion were past.

Six months ago, it'd finished! Finished – how could it finish; such love, such desire and need for a fellow human being. She sighed quietly to herself and rested her chin on her hand and continued to gaze into the square. Memories came flooding back, and as usual, tears stung her eyes but then again, like always, she fought hard against them, gradually suppressing them.

"Here we are, dear," said a cheery voice, "your tea! You look frozen today – there's quite a nip in the air, isn't there? More like winter than autumn."

She turned and looked up. "Yes," she said, "quite a nip. Thank you for my tea, I need it."

"You look done in, dearie. I hope nothing's wrong?" the waitress looked at the woman, concerned. "You're not your usual self today, are you?"

"No," Helen replied, "not my usual self. Memories – you know, they haunt us sometimes, without our asking – catches one off guard, so to speak."

"Oo, I know what you mean, love, a real problem sometimes. Still, best not to dwell on them, only makes you morbid!"

With that she gently patted the woman on the back and scuttled off towards the corridor leading to the rest of the hotel. "Strange woman," she muttered to herself, her mind moving on to other matters. Nothing in order, a collection of jumbled thoughts and duties woven into the garish patterns and confused tapestry of her daily life. Back in the tea-room the woman smiled to herself, she picked up her tea and cupping it in her hands, continued to look out of the window and remember.

It was a year to the day since he'd first brought her here. It was raining then, and they'd laughed as they'd rushed into the tea-room, to be greeted by a log fire and immediate welcomes and invitations to sit by the fire and dry themselves. Her feet were cold and wet, he'd bent down and removed her shoes and stood them in the hearth.

"There, they'll soon dry. I can't believe I've kept you out in the cold all this time, talking to you, I must be mad, but you know I could talk to you for ages."

She remembered smiling up at him and noticing the steadfast way he looked at her. She noted the contours of his face and body; steel blue eyes beneath hooded lids, the straight nose and sculptured face, the strong, broad shoulders. His stance was purposeful, almost military.

"Well," he said, "has the cat got your tongue?"

"No," she said, laughing, "I'm just wondering whether you'll disappear in a puff of smoke. We've had such a lovely day together – such fun."

"I hope it's the first of many, that is, if everything goes to plan. I've got a lot to accomplish, which I can and will, if you're here to listen to me. Do you realise you're the only person I've ever felt at ease with enough to voice my thoughts to. Now, there's a confession." He smiled ruefully.

"I'm glad you've made it. Sometimes, it's good to let go and show the true person beneath the public facade we all put on."

"Wow, that's a bit profound isn't it, for a wet afternoon."

They both laughed. She tried to sound flippant but felt wistful and hurriedly averted her gaze, turning to look at the fire. She couldn't let her vulnerability display itself too soon. She wasn't ready, not yet.

She knew though, that soon, very soon, like his outpourings earlier, she would have to do the same – but not yet. How would she do it, along a tow-path, like today, getting soaked – no, that wasn't the way. It would have to be somewhere quiet, because she knew she'd shake uncontrollably.

Here was a man she believed she could trust and not be ridiculed or 'put down' by – someone who'd accept her, accept her insecurities, the incredible sadness of her past. She'd have to write things down in order, so that there'd be no misunderstanding, no tactlessness, no stupidity. She was woken from her reveries by a gentle hand on her shoulder and a cup of tea being offered to her. She turned to take the cup and looked into eyes searching into hers for answers to unasked questions.

"I'm sorry," she said, "I was miles away."

"I know," he said, "where were you? You were so still, I thought I'd lost you for good."

She smiled at him, "Thank you for my tea." The scent of it assailed her nostrils, "How did you know I liked Earl Grey? You must be psychic."

"I don't know," he paused, "but I feel I've always known you. It's very daunting, but I feel safer than ever before in the company of a fellow human being. I've never known myself in this position before; it's actually rather more dangerous than I could have imagined. I've known extreme fear and danger with my job, but these feelings you've aroused in me are totally different and unknown; that's why I use the word dangerous. Can you understand?"

"I think so."

She didn't dare voice her own thoughts, which were so in tune with his.

If she had, she would have lost control and besides, today belonged to him, not to her. He had poured out his thoughts, his ambitions, and his dreams in a way she felt he'd never been able to do so before; she felt humbled and privileged at the experience and grateful to have been trusted enough to be told. It was only five weeks since they'd met, but in that time a bond had developed between them that was already strong.

"You understand me all right – of that I've no doubt – but where are you now?" he laughed. "You've gone again!"

"If I tried to explain, you'd probably laugh at me, call me stupid – most people do."

"I'm not most people – try me," he said gently.

She turned and looked at him; he handed her a piece of cake, his eyes dancing mischievously.

"Have some Madeira, m'dear," he joked. She laughed and took the cake.

"La, sir," she mimicked, "would you have me undone?"

"Faith, ma'am, you do read my thoughts too well!" he replied with mocking dignity, his attitude trying to hide the desire to find the woman beneath the closed exterior. But no chink appeared in her reserve – she remained an enigma to him. Perhaps for today he would let it ride, but something inside told him of the passion and feelings that were concealed so well.

He needed to know her, he wanted to know her, he couldn't allow life and all its problems to overshadow this desire for her – a completeness of feeling he'd never felt before. His mind criss-crossed across his past as he tried to analyse his feelings then with now, but they had been different, they weren't like this, here was something new something warm and enveloping. He found himself suddenly serious, the prospect of what might be daunting him.

"How's the cake?" his tone was clipped and cool.

She started at the sudden change in his voice, but remained calm and matched his tone with her, "Thank you, fine." He noted her restraint, his mind at once again alert to her, he began to question in his mind…who had hurt so badly that she should be on the defensive so much? He looked at her, but again there was nothing to detect in her face, she responded to his look with a nervous smile.

"This cake is very good; why don't you have some?"

He declined and she continued eating, quietly looking into the fire. She was suddenly aware that most of the customers had gone and looked at the emptying room anxiously.

"I'm sorry, I'm taking too long, perhaps we should go, and everyone else seems to have gone." She hurriedly replaced the plate and finished her tea.

"It's all right," he said, "there's no rush." He reached down and picked her shoes up from the hearth. "Look, they've dried, I think you'll be able to put them on again."

He bent down and lifted her foot, suddenly he turned and looked at her.

Her eyes were alive and large – she, like him, had sensed the power in his touch – the electricity between them. He held her gaze, determined not to see her turn away again. This time he needn't have worried, this time she held his gaze too, unspoken words and feelings instinctively there, and flashing between them.

"I won't be long."

He got up and went out into the foyer of the hotel to pay the bill, leaving her to try and calm herself. She watched him go – would the light-hearted friendship still be there when he returned? Everything had suddenly moved on – too fast; she knew she wasn't ready – it was too soon since…since…William…why should she remember him? He'd been a bastard, taken her for a ride, drained her of all trust and belief in men, and now here she was again trying not to let life move her on into yet another disastrous relationship and failing miserably. But, why should this new friendship not be different? She dismissed William immediately, he was the past and a memory not needed. Her thoughts returned to this present man, and she saw that he was coming back; valiantly she tried to regain composure by wriggling into her damp shoes.

"How about one for the road?" he said, "The bar's open."

"All right, if you like, I'll have a tomato juice."

She was surprised how flippant she sounded and how confident her voice was, "Thank God," she said to herself, "I'm back to normal; after all, it was nothing but a touch." She stood up and moved to him, he gently guided her towards the bar.

"Tomato juice, ice and lemon and make mine a whisky and water, please…"

That was the beginning. The beautiful unhurried, uncluttered beginning – no one hurt, no pain, no deceit. Two weeks later he'd gone back to his international life. He'd taken her out to lunch the day before he left and again they'd talked, but this time it was her turn to tell him of her ambitions, her desires. He listened patiently, studied her for the first time; her mouth – it was full and rounded, he saw too, her eyes, a deep blue. He indulged himself looking at her, without her glasses she saw him as a blur. He revelled in this as now he was able to command her gaze and see her eyes dance with fire, with the vision of life the more animated she became. Her face was young again, the strain and pain of life disappearing the more she spoke, the lines of bitter disappointment and frustration of the past gradually eradicated. She was not beautiful, but she was handsome through her innocent and optimistic acceptance of life, her gentle sensitivity and courageous belief in never giving in or taking 'no' for an answer. His eyes scanned her face again and rested on her lips – he longed to kiss them, to enfold her in his arms and feel the warmth of her body against his, her electricity pulsate through his body.

He noticed her hands, they were white. The nails unkempt, the skin dried.

Her vulnerability made him long to protect her, heal her in some way, but how? Suddenly, she stopped talking…

"I'm sorry, I've been talking too long, and you must be bored stiff." She hurriedly hid her hands under the table.

"You're not boring, and stop apologising – you're you! Come on, give me your hand." He stretched out his hand and smiled at her. It was such a re-assuring gesture, she hesitated, she longed to touch him, but couldn't.

"Fine," he said, "if you won't do as I ask, I'll take you for a walk and then I'll hold your hand. I want to go down to the marshes and see if the geese have flown in yet, that way I'll know whether or not it's cold in Russia."

He helped her into her coat and together they walked out towards his car.

He opened the door for her, and she slid into the deep leather seat, luxuriating in the comfort. She cared for her own car but this was real care, it even smelt good! He settled himself beside her, and deftly drove out of the small car park and onto the road towards the marshes.

"All right?" he asked.

"Yes, thank you," she replied, smiling back at him.

"Soon be there. By the way, do you know anything about the birds on the marshes?"

"No, I'm afraid not, my education is sadly lacking. I only know about boats, listening to the shrouds slapping against the masts and watching them ride at anchor."

"Good, I'll teach you, I often come and walk on the marshes, there's always something new to see. You're a terrible romantic, aren't you? All this talk about boats etc.... I can see I'm going to have to re-educate you before you get badly hurt."

"You don't have to tell me – it's something in me and I'm well aware of it."

He smiled and rested his hand briefly on hers. "Don't change; I enjoy hearing you paint pictures with words – it's rather endearing. Right, here we are," he peered through the windscreen, "and no geese!"

They scanned the coastline and sky, looking to see whether the specks on the horizon were the first of the winter migrators, but they were just sea birds fishing. He locked the car and carefully tucked her arm through his, and together they walked towards the marsh, past boats already on their winter moorings – tidily covered against the storms of the coming season. There was no one about, they had the marshes to themselves. He showed her animal and bird tracks – he named the paw prints of small mammals, the imprints of claws and webbed-footed birds; even the grasses and sea plants he could name. She was enthralled and absorbed everything he told her with enthusiasm. All too soon their time was up and they returned to the car.

"It's now my time to apologise," he said, "I must take you home – I've a lot to do before I leave tomorrow."

"I understand," she replied, "I've had a marvellous time – thank you."

"May I ask you something?" He looked carefully at her and then, when she said nothing, he continued, "I want to kiss you – I've wanted to for some time...but now it's important."

He looked down at her, searching her face for acquiescence. She nodded and waited for him to put his arms around her. Slowly, he lifted her face to his and bent and kissed her, gently at first but then with deepening passion as he felt her mouth part under his and their tongues explore one another. She allowed herself to cling to him, holding the lapels of his jacket, not wanting the moment to cease, feeling the power of his body, the warmth of his arms around her, the utter protection and safety of him. She found herself relaxing into him, and the more he felt the contours of her body against him, the more he tightened his hold on her.

He began to realise more and more how much he wanted her, to caress and kiss her naked body and possess her completely. Finally, she allowed herself to let go, knowing how much she wanted to know him, his body – to adore him, to feel the ecstasy of him in her – the life-giving force flood and overwhelm her. They clung together for some time until they gazed at each other with joy and burgeoning love, their radiance reflected in their faces – a look of happiness and hope expressed in their eyes.

He opened the car door for her and slowly she sank into the seat – kissing her again before leaving her for his side of the car. He steered the car out onto the road and turned towards her home. She leant across and touched his hand, feeling his fingers open and close over hers and seeing him smile at her touch. All too soon they were home, neither having spoken a word, each lost in their own thoughts, each trying to analyse their own turmoil within... Some days later, in the middle of the night the phone rang. It was him – clear as a bell from Russia. She still had a childlike surge of excitement whenever the phone rang from abroad – it was so easy now, not like the old days, when you booked a call hours in advance and waited for the operator to ring back. Then it was an event, now it was a matter of course...and here he was...sounding as if he were in the next room, not thousands of miles away.

"I have a confession to make to you..." the voice said, her heart sank. 'Now it comes, now the I'm-sorry bit,' she said to herself. The voice continued, "I'm in love with you," – slowly, the negative fog in her mind cleared as she absorbed the words...was it true what she'd heard, could she really believe them, or had half waking befuddled her mind and she'd heard wrongly? She started to tremble, how was she to describe the feelings stirred by such words, how can anyone not recognise the beauty and warmth, that first moment of feeling of knowing, of belonging to a fellow human being. Joy overwhelmed her as she slid down the bed and into the soft pillows, "Oh," she said softly, the voice continued.

"Are you there, can you hear me...oh, damn these phones..."

"Of course, I can hear you, I'm just...I don't know how to reply to you...my heart's pounding like anything...no one has ever told me they...love me...not once...I don't understand..." her voice trailed away...for a brief moment she wanted the phone to go dead so that she could savour the sweetness of the last few minutes… Emotion and hope overwhelmed her too much, it made her breathe heavily…he heard her.

"What's the matter…?" he asked, "I'm still here, talk to me… I'm always going to be beside you. I can't do without you. I need you too much, we have a great adventure ahead of us. My work is difficult, but with you near me, I can continue. Please tell me you need me too."

There was a pause, "Yes," she said, "I need you. I haven't dared voice my feelings or even admit to them, because I've never felt this way before, never woken up each morning and seen sunshine – even when skies are leaden and full of rain. I've never known joy, I've never known what it is not to breathe properly because of such a full heart…" she paused and then suddenly all the suppressed love of past years, of emotions condemned to conventional behaviour welled up in her and she blurted out… "I need you, I long for you. At night my body aches for you, there isn't a fibre in my being that doesn't cry out your name, each minute, each hour, each day. I cannot imagine my life without you. If you were to go, I'd wander aimlessly, devoid of sensibility and rational thought.

"There'd be no tears. A void of nothingness would exist where feelings once were. I am in you as you are in me – no matter where you are, I believe that we are bound irrevocably to each other. I love too, and now believe I am loved as well."

There was a pause and then his voice steady and clear, so full of supressed passion, spoke quietly across the miles of land and sea that separated them.

"Yes, you are loved – deeply loved. A dangerous word, so often abused. I vowed never to use it – but I have. I'll be home in two days, meet me at Heathrow. I'll tell you my flight details when I ring you tomorrow.

"Goodnight my darling, I'll imagine you asleep – and in my imaginings I'll kiss your eyes, your face, your hair, your body and protect you."

"Say again what you said to me earlier – please let me hear you say it again so that I know this has not been a beautiful dream," her voice was tremulous.

"I am falling in love with you; I am in love with you."

"Thank you," she said, "thank you for loving someone like me, for who I am and not for what I ought to be. Goodnight, my love, and come safely back."

The phones went dead – that particular cord was severed, but the new cord now between them was strong and intact. She lay back on the pillows and tried to think and take control of the turmoil in her mind, the 'why me' and the answer 'why not me?' kept coming back, disrupting the logic of clear thought she was trying to regain. In the end, tiredness took control and hugging her lovely memories to herself, she slept…

"Madam," a voice of cold reality and the present brought her out of her reverie, "your tea's cold, would you like some more…? And if you keep hold of that cup like that, it'll break and then where will you be?"

She turned and looked up, and Annie saw the pain etched on the woman's face. She carefully put the cup down and smiled up at her. "I'm sorry, I'm really not myself today, am I? I don't seem to want anything – not even your Madeira cake, and I always look forward to that."

"Well, sometimes we don't always feel like eating, do we? It's something to do with hormones, I believe. Well, that's what they say about women of a well, you know…" Annie suddenly looked at the woman and realised that her remarks were getting personal, so she added simply, "Have you finished now, shall I clear it?"

"Yes, thank you, I've finished," she smiled to herself at Annie's sharpness.

"There's a lovely fire in the bar – go and have your usual, Bill's behind tonight and he'll be pleased to see you." She started collecting the china onto the tray, the woman watched her for a moment and wished that she too could dismiss memories to the recesses of her mind and accept the mundanity of life with such ease – but she couldn't – perhaps it was 'hormones' as Annie said.

She picked up her bag and said goodbye and walked towards the bar. It was warm, the firelight danced on the wood panelling and lamps threw out rancid colour from beneath smoke-covered shades, pools of light spread across the floor, spilling onto the deep reds and greens of the rugs in front of the fire, creating spectrums of colour and invitations to indulge in the ambience.

She moved to the fire and spread her hands, grateful for the warmth and dancing shadows.

"Hello love, nice to see you. Will you have your usual?"

She nodded without turning and called over her shoulder, "Yes please, but no ice tonight – it's too cold."

"Right-oh!" came the cheery reply, "You stay where you are, I'll bring it over to you." She sat by the fire and returned to her musings. Figures presented themselves to her in the embers – faded dreams and hopes paraded in front of her – the hurts and torments became intrusive, her mind raced and again the tears stung her eyes. Why, why could she not forget, why must she be reminded all the time? When would the hurt stop, sanity be restored again?

"Here you are, love, stay and warm yourself – this'll do you good." He looked into the woman's face, worry spread across his features at the contortions of pain in her eyes. "You look all in."

"Funny, Annie said the same earlier. I think I must be suffering from the cold." She smiled at him, grateful for the look of concern on his face – it was reassuring – a lifeline in this never-ending agony of bewilderment and loss. "Thank you Bill, I'll enjoy this very much." She forced a smile of gratitude, he nodded and left the glass on the table.

She picked up the glass and watched the firelight dance in the amber liquid, so many times before she'd done this…but in the past he'd been there – the warmth of their stolen nights together, their passion and joy in the physical contact with each other so willingly so completely…so gently given. This was no carnal lust…they had stood before each other naked, enveloping themselves with serenity and peace, their desire in giving so deep – the exquisite ecstasy of final intimacy reaching out into their very souls, touching the very fibres of their being. She had never known before the power of intense physical closeness with another human being, the abandonment of natural thought and will in the bliss of giving. They had lain for what seemed hours in each other's arms, their hearts racing! Slowly subsiding into natural rhythm, neither talking nor wanting to leave the other. And so it had continued, these stolen times, each time more beautiful, more exhilarating, each completion a feeling of wonder and peace…

She suddenly remembered that awful day when that word was used, WIFE! He had one! He'd deceived her, he'd destroyed her with one word that related to another human being. She wondered – did she have feelings too? He'd assured her there was nothing between them now, no physical contact, just an existence out of duty – "too many years together, you know. I must try and make things better for the sake of my work and children, nothing unsavoury must interfere with that, but when that's settled…who knows…" For a brief time she'd trusted his judgement, accepted his arguments, but then he'd told her his wife had found out. Panic had become his watchword, fear and loss of status his guide. Finally, he'd gone again but not without coming and telling her, "It's over. I must try and make my marriage work for the sake of my children, my job; I've too much to lose! You do understand, don't you? I'm sorry…"

How can anyone accept or understand such words so callously delivered? Shock, disbelief, sickening, sinking feelings engulf and surge through mind and body. Hurt, deep, deep hurt born of betrayal of intimate trust of one human being for another, for their well-being, their life, surfaces and spreads with silent death across the sea of emotional tranquillity. Minutes pass, then hours, then days and constantly the question 'why' is asked. Tears, unrelenting tears numb the senses and the mind loses coherence to normal thought. Actions become robotic duties, but always Desolation and Despair are constant companions. Sleep becomes an opiate of desire and relief from the unrelenting burden of these two, and their tortuous claws of grief.

So it was with her – friends had rallied, invitations had been offered and advice proffered – but to no effect. Life was mechanical and this living bereavement had to be played out – but for how long and would the pain ever cease? Would she ever be the happy person she once was? Doubtful – she longed for a time, perhaps a year into the future, when memories would have become dim reflections of a beautiful interlude. She knew her 'preservation' each week, of tea, a drink and the 'one for the road' payment into the pot was destructive, but the time was not yet here to move on, the road of barren nothingness stretched ahead and had to be walked to its ultimate end. Even now in the depths of despair, hope was sometimes there, telling her that tomorrow was another day – and perhaps, just perhaps there were the beginnings of an easing of pain and a belief in the future; logical answers and understanding dawning as to his behaviour. But love, the need, the desire for him, would never leave her.

The fire that had been kindled all those months ago still glowed, the embers of constancy and loyalty for every aspect of him as great now as ever. One word and they would flame into life imbuing hope, reducing illusory Despair and Desolation to ashes.

She remembered the letter she'd written in the middle of the night – phrases came back to her but she'd not had the emotional strength to re-read them – but now, the letter was in her handbag still. Quietly and purposefully, she reached down and took it out – the lines blurred in front of her, so many of them, so many words, such jumbled thoughts…but still she would read and try and extinguish the ghost of raw feelings that caused her to write so long ago.

"Because you're so far away, I find myself writing to you from my heart.

"I am so lost without you, not hearing your voice or feeling your arms around me…'

She paused and drank – 'So far so good,' she thought, the word 'mobile' sprang off the page and the phrase "I heard your voice," then on "but you didn't hear me – the line went dead and you were gone, but for a brief second you were with me again." She remembered vividly that call, the frustration of 'no contact', the anonymity of the mechanical voice 'there is a fault'. On down the page she read, the intensity of it starting to affect her… "I sound so selfish wanting you here with me…I lack the lustre for life without you somewhere near…I'm gradually coming to terms…your marriage to work…I was merely an interlude…" the list was endless, she paused and drank again, finding courage in the liquid to carry on. "I'm sorry not just for me, who fell in love with you, but for you because I was such a catalyst to your own dormant feelings; you knew and gave again passion and pursued happiness with such fervour and all it has caused is pain and distress to us and your wife. I feel for her…" So it continued, an assuaging of guilt on her part, an apology to the wife – the faceless being that suffered too, and still the questions came back that she'd asked before. Is a so-called happiness in reconciliation just another way out because of duty to time and responsibilities?

Are his wife's tears merely feelings of anger at seeing her 'possession' taken away – her security denuded before her? After all this time she still had no answer. Was she still so innocent, so accepting in her honesty that if something is wrong between people, cure it? Isn't it kinder to release one from the bonds and sanctity of a piece of paper?

She'd always been ready to put the happiness of others above her own wishes – it was something inherent in her, she saw no reason for any creature, either animal or human, to suffer, but it seemed that her childlike belief in this was a curse. She raised the glass to her lips and moved her feet closer to the fire, the comfort of it and the peaceful crackling of the logs warmed her. She turned back to the letter and read the final paragraph, "I know you to be an honourable man but sometimes we make false assumptions by being disloyal to ourselves and denying the existence of our true feelings. By listening to the inner voices, clarity of thought becomes simple…"

So it went on, precious phrases that reminded her of the night she'd written them, the torment that had filled her mind, and the only release – to write them down. She turned back to the page and read the last entry "…wherever you are, wherever you go, I will always be with you."

She let the letter fall into her lap and continued looking into the fire. The words were as true now as when she'd first written them all those confused months ago. She was still deeply in love with him, there was no doubt in her mind – but was it wise to continue to live a possible dream or be practical? Probably the latter, but she was a romantic and optimism and faith in miracles had always been the stronger pull. She sighed and returned the letter to her bag, stood up and put on her coat, staring into the fire one last time.

Her mobile rang, and reality intruded – the message was short – could she be in London tomorrow for a meeting at ten? She replied in the affirmative, resignation registering in her voice. She had become fond of this little town and the idea of going away from it, for whatever reason, annoyed her, still it was her job and that had to come first before anything else; besides, being able to work from home made her occasional trips to London an enjoyable adventure, so where was the harm?

She gathered up her things and left the cosy security of the fire and moved to the bar.

"Thanks, Bill, you were right. It was good and it did warm me. By the way, will you put this away for me…?" she handed some money across the counter, "…in the usual place, for a large double with water, please?"

Bill took the money and placed it in the tankard above the bar. "You know there's quite a tidy sum in the pot now. How long do you want me to keep it for you?"

"Just a little while longer, perhaps another month, please."

"Are you sure it'll be needed?"

"Yes, it'll be needed." she replied emphatically.

"Forgive me, miss…but who do I say left it and how will I, er, know them?" Unease showed on his face as he stammered out his request.

"Just say 'a friend' if you're asked, but you'll know because he'll want 'one for the road', and it'll always be a double whisky and water."

After a pause she smiled and went on, "He made a great impression on me and left an indelible mark on my life – if you like this is a sort of thank you, nothing more."

Bill nodded, 'Shame they've not kept in touch,' he thought to himself; he muttered "Goodnight" and returned to polishing the counter and straightening the mats. She said goodbye and slipped quietly away from the warmth of the bar and into the cold of early evening. He watched her go, before disappearing to the cellars. After a time he returned, failing to notice the man immersed in a paper in the corner; the paper was lowered and the man moved to the bar.

"Good evening sir, I'm sorry I didn't notice you. What can I get you?"

"One for the road, please…a double whisky and water."

Bill started and looked clearly at the man, steel blue eyes met his and a faint smile flickered around his mouth.

'Certainly, sir," refusing the man's money, "there's no need to pay, it has been done for you." He pointed up at the shelf behind him. The man's eyes followed and then looked back at Bill; quietly he asked,

"Who left it?"

"A lady, she didn't give her name, but comes in here each week at the same time and asks to leave this money for a double whisky and water. I asked her who it was for and how I'd know them and she said, 'Just tell them a friend left it and it will always be the same thing, one for the road – large double whisky with water'." Hesitatingly he asked, "I presume it is you?"

"Yes, it's me," he paused, "how long's she been coming?"

"As I said, once a week…for the last six months…she has tea first and then comes in here by the fire and has a drink."

"And it's always a Tuesday?"

"Yes, sir, always a Tuesday."

Bill watched as the man returned to his chair with his drink. Bill smiled to himself, intrigued at the story seemingly unfolding, 'Annie will be in her element when she hears what I've got to tell her!'

Chapter 9

"Come along, love, time to wake up now. You can't sit here sleeping your life away anymore. The family's all here and I've already had a G and T, John really does make an awfully good 'snifter'. Now, what about it? Are you ready to face the fray?"

He bent down and removed the blanket that had been put over her and folded it up. Helen sleepily looked at him and a warm glow enveloped her, what a joy this man was and how much he meant to her. Life would have been so very tough in her later years if he'd never come into her life, every day she thanked the 'Great Spirit' for his companionship and love. What a change he'd been after all the 'hardness' of the past, but now all that had faded, distant memories too horrid to even contemplate or think about. Life with this man had been wonderful, full of adventure, people from many faiths and cultures, different countries, different lives, nothing parochial or banal.

She stretched, "Sorry dear, I've had so many dreams, about our past, as well as others unfortunately not wanted, funny how they can still raise their ugly heads. Anyway, I'm now more than ready to meet everyone but first, I'll check my 'looks' and then a very large 'snifter' for me too."

He took her hand and helped her up, she was getting rather stiff these days, but once up all her old strength flowed and she was off! He smiled and gave her a kiss, "Off you go, but don't be too long, by the way you look good, so not much war paint needed."

"You old flatterer, I'm glad your eyes are failing a bit, you no longer see my blemishes, I'll be back soon."

"My eyes aren't failing, it's just the light that's bad, always has been in this house." He drew himself up to his full height and stood with military precision in front of her, "I know when my wife looks good and it's now, and I don't need to be told any differently." He smiled at her and watched as she disappeared out of the room; he turned to the fire and stoked it up again, putting the guard in front and waited for her to return.

"That's better, will I do?" she said, posing coquettishly in front of him.

"You know you will, now come along and stop putting ideas into my head."

He playfully tapped her backside and opened the door and together they walked into the hub of the home and family. Helen was hugged and kissed by what seemed an army of people, all anxious to speak to her and tell her their news.

"I really can't speak to any of you yet until I've had a drink. My throat is as dry as tinder, will someone please give me a drink, and not just a wet glass!"

Laughter ensued and a large glass of wine was dutifully put into her hand by her step-son, who bent to talk to her,

"There you are, Helen, may I call you that now? I feel anything else is a bit old hat; I'm no longer the lanky youth you first knew but a married man with children of my own. You've never met my wife, so come and say 'hello'. Linda and I met in America, New York to be precise." He helped her to her feet and took her across the room to where his wife and the children were talking to her step-daughter, Meg. "Linda, this is my step-mother, Helen; Helen, this is my wife and these are our children."

Meg kissed her step-mother and gave her a hug, Helen responded and looked at Linda and took in her dark eyes, glossy hair and olive skin, the girl put out her hand.

"Hello, I'm so pleased to meet you, I'm sorry I've never met you before."

"Don't be, now's the right time to meet and to get to know you and your children; what are their names?"

John stepped in, "The eldest is Charlotte, I hope you don't mind, but I wanted to name her after your daughter, my step-sister, I never knew her for long but what I did know, I liked very much."

Helen looked at the child and noticed that she had the same coloured hair and large hazel eyes of her own long dead child, the little girl took Helen's hand and smiled, "My name's really Sarah, Charlotte's my middle name, and this is my brother Thomas, he's shy so won't speak but he will soon."

Helen shook the little hand carefully and said, "I'm so glad to meet you Sarah Charlotte, and you too, Thomas, perhaps we'll read a story together sometime." There was a nod and a retreat back to their mother's skirt. Helen turned to John,

"What a kind thing to do, I'm touched; you know, Sarah's got her eyes. I'm so pleased to see them both and your wife too, she's very bonny." Helen looked at John's wife and the children as they stood talking with Meg,

"Linda's father is English and her mother's Malay; her parents met whilst working in Singapore, he's a doctor and she was a nursing sister in the same hospital. Linda is a paediatrician, quite high-powered and lecturing a lot. It's good as I'm often abroad these days and the children are happy in school, so our lives work well." His step-mother looked quizzically at him, "It's all right, Helen, we have very good child-care in New York for them both, but Sarah's in school all day now, so rarely needs the child-minder. I still like to keep her on though, I find it 'comforting' to know they're in good hands and the children adore her."

"I'm so glad. You really seem to have fallen on your feet. Do you remember the terrible fights we had with your father over your leaving school and going to college? But you were right and we were wrong in trying to influence you, and now look at you, a successful scientist with your own family. I'm so proud."

She turned and smiled at him before going to talk with Meg and Linda. Meg linked her arm in her stepmother's and Helen was content. She'd always had a soft spot for Meg and often found her easier to talk to than her own daughter; Meg said it was because she was 'looking in' and not 'immediately connected'. 'Perhaps she was right,' Helen thought, 'there was no blood between them.' Even so, she wished there was more rapport with her daughter; she knew she'd left Sophie too much to her own 'devices' and that inevitably she'd turned and formed a deep friendship with an old friend, Susan, who'd become her 'surrogate mother'. Helen was hurt then, still was, now, after all these years. She should have made more time for the girl and not allowed Susan to 'creep in', but grief and bewilderment at that time had been confusing. In Helen's mind, provided Sophie was loved and cared for, all would be well; simplistic, yes, but the child's happiness and a return to normality had been uppermost in her mind and love most of all. She'd never stopped loving her despite the barrier between them both, but now the past was a long time ago and her shortcomings must be forgotten. NOW was a new time and new beginnings within the family, she must look forward with hope. She looked around the room and saw Sophie talking avidly with Lucy, a tea towel in her hand, each of them gesticulating frantically at the table, obviously deciding where everyone was to sit; there were twenty of them tonight around the old family table. Twenty, where had they all come from? Heaven knows, but Helen loved family gatherings and this was to be one in a million. Lucy had decreed that there was to be a big family party tonight of all nights and she'd got her wish; "Close family and three very old friends of Grannie and Grumps, plus Mum's old friend Susan and her husband Tony."

"May I call you Helen, please?" Helen returned to normal and looked at Linda,

"Of course you may, I've now met another member of my extended family and I'm delighted. You've no idea how much it all means to me, and look over there at Grumps, absolutely engrossed with John and Tony, Susan's husband, and it looks like he's got another drink, he'll snore like a trooper tonight!"

Meg said, "Why's he called 'Grumps', it doesn't suit him you know, he's never grumpy."

Helen laughed, "It's on account of a newspaper article he read years ago, don't ask me to remember it, but it put him in a foul mood all day and Sophie's husband took him down to the pub for a drink and came up with the name and it's stuck ever since. I think he quite likes it, a sort of badge of office so to speak."

"I'm looking forward to talking to Grumps," said Linda, "I believe he knew Malaya well, you were both there weren't you, Helen?"

"I'm afraid I was there for a very short period, there were troubles which escalated and all wives were sent home as a precaution; but yes, do speak to him, he's full of stories, I keep wanting him to write them down but he says, no, he hasn't time. I suggest you take a tape recorder with you, or whatever they're called these days, and see what you can get down, even I'd be interested."

At that moment there was a tap on a glass and everyone became silent. Grumps was helped onto a stool and raised his glass, "Unaccustomed as I am…" there was a groan from all in the room, he smiled and continued, "I've said it once, so won't repeat," a kindly buzz rippled around the room, they all liked Grumps, "As I'm now the elder statesman of this family, I think some toasts are in order, the first is to the bride-to-be, Lucy, may your life beginning tomorrow be full of fun and laughter and not too many tears, and I'd like to be a great-grandfather before I die, if possible but not mandatory, but for now enjoy the new adventure that's starting. So, all of you, raise your glasses to Lucy," they cheered and drank Lucy's health, she smiled back at them all and looked embarrassed.

Grumps continued, "And now to our host and hostess, Sophie and Ian, for looking after us and feeding us like fighting cocks, and for producing such delightful young people in Lucy and Paul." Again there were cheers and laughter and glasses refilled and toasts drunk.

"Finally, to us all and my adopted family. May we meet again in the future many times and may good fortune be always with us, but when misfortune does hit, may we always be there to help one another." A chorus of "hear, hear" coupled with drinking and happy talk ensued, broken by the interjection of Ian's summoning them all to table.

The table looked spectacular, full of flowers, family silver and the inevitable candles; Lucy's face was a picture of happiness as she carefully sat everyone down where she wanted them to be. Helen and Grumps were placed at either end of the table and everyone else arranged around them, Sophie as usual, sat near to the kitchen door, with Meg and Lucy near her to help, Ian was near to Helen and Paul wanted to be near Grumps. Lucy decided that after each course the men should move one place to the left and the girls two places to the right, there was much confusion and laughter and as the meal went on and the drink flowed, people forgot their numbers and which way they were supposed to go, but it didn't matter, this was the 'Family' and precious moments were captured forever in the fun and games that ensued. Luckily, Helen and Grumps were told to sit still, they just met the different guests as they came and sat beside them and enjoyed the general chatter. Finally, Helen's greatest friend, Vicky, arrived beside her, by then it was the last course and the two friends remained companionably content. Vicky had always been there for Helen with logical advice and Helen for Vicky. Vicky's life had been anything but easy but she'd forged a life for herself which had been completely selfless and her works for the benefit of others had been relentless. She, like Helen, had had disastrous marriages, but where one had been terminated through mental cruelty, the other one she'd tolerated and forged this life of 'giving' to expunge her empty home life.

"Well, my dear, what a gathering! Everyone so happy, I'm delighted to be here."

"I couldn't imagine your not being here," said Helen, "You've been my rock for so many years, I'd be mortified not to have you near me."

"We have been through a lot, you and I, haven't we? But here we are towards the ends of our lives and now happy. Would you have changed anything about the past, now looking back?"

"Apart from the death of Charlotte and my deep-seated hurt over Susan's relationship with Sophie, no, I don't think I would. I always remember the old Rector talking to me after Charlotte's death and telling me that, 'He only gives life-changing problems to those that are strong enough to accept them.' Heavy, I know, but when you think back, you and I are strong, look at the abuse and lack of affection you've tolerated, years and years of it, but still you've gone on and done so much for others with no thought for yourself, now that's what I call unselfishness that goes beyond bounds. As for Susan, well, that's a thorn I know, but I wonder if it's ever done any real harm? I don't know, after all, Sophie is still my flesh and blood. I know one thing though," Helen said ruefully, "I'm not sharing a pew tomorrow with Susan like I did for Sophie's wedding; I want you, and all of 'us', to be behind Sophie and Ian as I know she and Tony will automatically be with them. I'd like to retain some pride and enjoy watching Lucy and Nick! Heavens, just had a thought, thank goodness I don't have to sing again! At least that's one thing I can thank 'age' for."

They both laughed at that, Vicky said,

"Yes, that must be a relief, going back to Susan, she has been a bit of an infringement, I grant you, and I still don't understand why she's never realised what she's put you through, and your losing Charlotte as well; you'd think she'd have 'backed off' or at least been more of a friend to you. To this day I don't understand your daughter's attitude, has she never realised the hurt she's put you through?"

"No, I think she's just thought 'It's Mother, being theatrical and jealous for no reason', nothing more. Her life has been too full of business, her little family and Susan's to think otherwise. I have to admit she's been a brilliant mother to Paul and Lucy and that's really all that's mattered. Still, the human psyche is very odd, but I don't want to dwell on 'past wrongs'; tomorrow we'll have a ball!"

Soon the meal was finished, and they all went into the drawing-room, the young and Lucy disappeared into the kitchen, saying they'd 'clear up'. Lucy smiled and followed them, carrying a couple of bottles and glasses with her. Sophie saw her mother and smiled at her,

"I suppose the glasses will survive and your china, I've given them strict instructions what to do."

"Don't even think about it, it was a lovely meal and now come and relax for a bit, because you won't be relaxing anymore for the next two days." Helen put her arm around her daughter and gave her a hug. At that moment Susan emerged from the kitchen and suddenly linked her arm through Helen's, the latter froze, 'Now what?' She seemed very merry.

"I hope you'll sit by me in church tomorrow, just like the last time, it'll be nice for the four of us to be together, now we have Tony and Grumps with us too."

Helen carefully extricated herself and held Susan's hand, and thought, 'Insensitive to the end.'

"No, I don't think so, I'm going to be behind with my elderly friends, besides there won't be enough room in the front, particularly as Lucy wants the dogs there too, I think you'll have more than enough to do with Sophie, controlling them."

"Oh, what a shame, I was so hoping that…" Susan's voice tailed off. Helen gave her a quick peck on the cheek, she'd quietly put her in her place, she smiled and went into the drawing-room, Sophie and Susan watching her go.

Grumps greeted her with another glass of wine and soon they were both surrounded by their friends and talking. Half an hour later, Lucy and Paul came into the room carrying a tray with tea and hot chocolate, they were greeted with murmurs of delight at the sight of another drink, albeit non-alcoholic, and Lucy was treated to comments of "Well, last night of home comforts," and "Get a good night's sleep" etc., and Paul to with "Will we see your girlfriend tomorrow?" and "Will you be next and when?" The two took everything in good humour and laughed and told jokes; Linda and John returned, having put the children to bed, and joined in. Meg returned too, with Paul and Sammy, her two children by her previous marriage, from the kitchen. The children went and poured their mother a hot chocolate, with marshmallows on top, and themselves tea plus a handful of marshmallows each!

"They won't go to bed, and as it's a very special weekend, I'm sure no one will mind if they stay up, and, yes, very fattening I know, but I love hot chocolate and marshmallows."

"Why not, I like the idea of us all being together; after all, when will it happen again?"

"Who knows, might be me next time," Meg said cynically, she saw Helen's face, "No, not a hope!"

Helen felt deflated, she so wanted Meg to be happy, she loved her very much, always thought of her as her intelligent step-daughter with bouncy puppy habits, just like her dog, Boogie, a cock-a-poo. She and the dog had stayed with Helen and Grumps many times and each time it had been delightful, Grumps enjoying good-natured arguments with her and all of them walks together.

Sophie and Susan and the rest of the company came into the room and settled down with tea and hot chocolate too and the time passed too quickly. Lucy had suddenly demanded 'charades' and despite some groans, they'd all joined in and half who guessed and were put in to 'play' forgot was it a film, or was it a play, had it been made into a film, but had soldiered on, miming the sections carefully, some, particularly the elderly friends, forgetting what they'd first thought about and having to be prompted which, of course, destroyed the charade, but it was still fun and reminded Helen of long ago house parties. She looked across the room and saw Vicky 'fading' and Grumps yawning. Stella and Noel and Peter and Tessa were starting to fade too but valiantly trying to keep going; however, her eye was caught.

"I'm sorry dears, but unless I get to bed, you'll have to carry me to the church or tell me about the wedding later on. I think the time has come for Grumps and I to retire to our couch, the clock's struck and it's a bit late for us now. It's been a wonderful evening, Lucy, well done you for deciding it and Sophie and Ian for preparing it, and tomorrow will be beautiful."

Helen and Grumps' friends got up thankfully and said their goodbyes, and kisses and hugs were exchanged and they were seen to the door and their cars. Luckily, they had very short distances to go and Helen thought, 'With long lie-ins, they'll be fine tomorrow.' She and Grumps waved them off and closed the front door. They went back into the drawing-room and said their goodnights, Sophie gave her mother a big hug, "Love you Mum," she whispered into her ear; she said the same to Grumps. Ian gave his mother-in-law a hug and kiss and patted his father-in-law's back, muttering a low "Thanks to you both, for everything." Helen and Grumps disappeared out of the room.

"Oh, I'm glad that's over, I'm so tired," said Grumps, "I'm wondering if I'll make the stairs to our room."

"Of course you will, come on lean on me, and we'll help each other."

Helen knew this was his way of getting his arm around her, something they'd always enjoyed, being tactile. Together they made their way to bed, commenting, as usual, on the comfort of the house and how nice it was to be here and how good it was to see the family and their friends and wondering what tomorrow's adventure would bring, and so with gentle chatting they were both soon in bed, reading their books prior to putting out the lights.

"Don't put the alarm on will you, dear, please?" implored Helen, "Just for once can we wake normally."

"But what about your tea? I must get that for you."

"No problem on that score, I've set the Teasmade for eight o'clock, you can have a rest, for a change I'll make it instead."

"Won't be the same," he muttered.

"Of course it won't, we're not at home at the moment, everything's different, so let me do the honours instead. Goodnight, love," she said, kissing him. "See you in the morning, sleep well."

He turned and kissed her, "Goodnight dear, see you then too." He turned and switched off the light and they slept... perchance to dream?

Chapter 10

The day dawned overcast. Helen got up and looked out of the window and watched the grey clouds scudding across the sky like foaming waves, shafts of blue being intermittently shown as tempters of what might be in store later on. She glanced down at the garden; though it had rained in the night, it didn't seem to have suffered too much, the roses were still upright and so were the delphiniums and lupins, the orange blossom's scent wafted up to her through the open window, and Cat could be seen lurking in the shrubbery, waiting for an unsuspecting dog to be let out. She'd bat its nose and then rub herself against its legs just to show who was in charge. Helen sighed, 'So all is normal,' she mused, 'the great day has dawned.' She turned and looked at her sleeping husband, dead to the world, one foot hanging out of bed from under the duvet. At that moment the Teasmade's alarm went off and the belching and gurgling of the boiling water started up and finally spluttered into the teapot itself. She didn't know why, but ever since she was introduced to a Teasmade, she'd always worried whether or not the water would flow into the pot or disgorge itself all over the tray instead, but no, all was well and her husband woke.

"Hello, dear," she said, bending down and giving him a kiss, "slept well?"

"Oh yes, my darling, now just come here and have a cuddle, the tea can wait." He pulled her down to him and gave her a massive kiss full on the mouth, "Now how's that for a wedding morning kiss?"

"Lovely," she curled up beside him and snuggled into his shoulder. "If our children could see us now, they'd be shocked, people of our age." She giggled and snuggled even further into him.

"Well, they're never going to know, are they? Now off you go and get me my 'tea in bed', woman, that I've been promised."

She rolled over off the bed and he playfully slapped her bottom, "Oo," she said and laughed at him and poured the tea. They both sat in bed and enjoyed the peace and a further cup of tea, before there was a knock at the door and Sophie looked in.

"Thank goodness you're all right; Lucy's been sick, Ian's got a thick head and Paul's feeling morose. Will you have a boiled egg for breakfast, I suggest we eat in about an hour at nine, the wedding people are coming at nine-thirty and the final flowers for the marquee at ten, then I've organised a buffet lunch of soup and salad at twelve-thirty before we all get changed. Hopefully, everything will run to plan, otherwise I'll still be getting ready on my way to church."

Helen and Grumps stared in disbelief at Sophie, her plans were well meant but the chances of their ever 'running to plan' were farfetched, Helen knew she'd chip a nail or ladder her stocking and be frantically doing running repairs whilst on the way to church, with the bridesmaids holding whatever was needed all the way there, but Sophie was her daughter and in any emergency that came along someone would be there to mend, as usual. Grumps looked at his step-daughter and thought how pleased he was to be going to the church, ahead of the 'final panics' with Paul, at least nothing would go wrong with their preparations and there'd be people at the church to talk to!

As fast as she'd appeared, Sophie disappeared, the whirlwind of organised chaos had left. Helen and Grumps looked at each other.

"Well, this morning's going to be fun, isn't it?" said Grumps, "I don't envy you your morning at all!"

"It's only nerves with Lucy, it'll soon pass. Ian's head will clear once he's eaten, Paul's mood will change later, and Sophie will look a picture perfect bride's mother and Lucy, well Lucy will be radiant and serene as soon as she's dressed and on her way to the church. Suddenly, it'll all be over and we'll be into the speeches and food and I'll be, thankfully, without my hat!"

Grumps looked at his wife and shook his head. "I so hope you're right." He got out of bed and was soon merrily showering in the bathroom, muttering happily away to himself. Helen poured another cup of tea and looked out of the window, the cat was still in the shrubbery and one of the dogs was getting awfully close to her, 'Any minute now there'll be an eruption' but strangely nothing, the cat emerged and rubbed herself against the dog and the two of them meandered up the garden to the kitchen door and breakfast.

Grumps appeared from the bathroom clean and ready to face the world, or at least the immediate world of his wife's day dreaming.

"Come on, old girl, get a move on, at least if we're down everything won't be overcooked and we'll eat in peace before the young emerge at all the wrong times and create further chaos. I'll go down now, hurry up and come down soon." He gave her a peck on the cheek and disappeared, his voice floating up from the garden a few moments later.

"Make mine five minutes please, your mother will be down in ten minutes, so don't put hers in yet." She looked out of the window and watched him walk down the garden to the potting shed with Ian, his hands gesticulating everywhere. The bedroom door opened and a pasty faced Lucy peered around,

"Hello love, how're you feeling?"

"Awful, Granny, how on earth can I be married looking like this and being so sick?"

"Simple, admit to yourself that you drank too much last night and that your suffering for it now, along with nerves at what's ahead of you today. This time tomorrow you'll be wondering what all the fuss was about; you'll be relaxing and we'll still be partying!"

"Do you really think I'm being sick because of nerves, heavens, that's a relief! I was beginning to think I'd got a bug." Helen looked at Lucy and was pleased to see that colour was beginning to flood back into her face and she smiled.

"Now, run along, Grumps has just told them I'll be down in ten minutes and five have gone already, I hate a spoiled breakfast, besides how can I come and talk to you if you're not dressed and ready for the hairdresser?"

"Oh heck, I'd forgotten her. OK, I'll go and leave you to it. See you later."

Helen watched her go and just for good measure locked the bedroom door and rushed into the bathroom for a shower. Just over five minutes later, she was washed and dressed and running down the stairs to the kitchen, entering it in her usual controlled manner and greeting everyone with a big grin.

"Come on, Gran, you can use my chair." It was Paul, in old trainers and tracksuit bottoms, an old tee shirt and scruffy hair and unshaven chin. Helen closed her eyes and raised her face to the ceiling, his unwashed body smelt heavily of sweat and testosterone, not too badly but enough to put her off her breakfast at nine in the morning!

"Thank you, Paul dear, now, are you going to shower?"

"Oh, do I smell?" he raised an arm and sniffed, Helen felt a little light-headed as the smell of his body was augmented, "I'd hoped I could get away with it until lunch time and then have a hot bath, obviously not." He looked at Helen, her face spoke volumes, he left the room. Sophie walked in with Helen's egg and toast and sniffed.

"I see Paul's been in and we now have the aroma of early twenties eau de body." She marched up to the kitchen door and flung it wide. "Sorry about that, Mum, but it'll soon dissipate, tea?"

"Yes please, I'd forgotten how pungent young men were first thing in the morning. In my day everyone was bathed and dressed by nine in the morning, I suppose it's quite a treat to be greeted by an unwashed body, I must remember it."

"Now, Mother, please no sarcasm or odd comments today, I've enough on my plate getting him to wear a suit, let alone a morning suit."

"Sorry dear, but it was rather an eye opener! Has Grumps eaten yet? If not where is he, we need to get this room cleared as soon as possible for you."

"Yes, he's done and is with Ian moving steps about for the wedding people. He's really entering into the spirit of today and having fun, can I ask you to be with Lucy for most of the morning? I know you're having your hair done later together, but I really could do with 'doing my own thing', if you understand me."

"'Course I do, but make sure that Grumps has a rest sometime this morning, just an hour, I've got to make sure he's not too tired at any time today, otherwise his medication won't work."

"Will do." Sophie sat down opposite her mother and poured tea and stuffed a piece of toast into her mouth. Breakfast was soon over and the table cleared, ready for the final flowers to be arranged. Helen laid the trolley in the corner for the lunch later on and watched as the final boxes and buckets were brought in, the scent was overpowering and within minutes the large table decorations for the marquee and top table were in place and being carried out to be arranged in situ. Helen wandered after them and for the first time saw the inside of the marquee, it was spectacular. Lucy and Sophie had opted for a blue and pink colour scheme and Helen gazed in wonder at the massive delphiniums and scabious and full-blown old-fashioned deep pink roses. From the crystal chandeliers hung balls of lavender and pink bud roses and all the pillars were wound around with pink and blue plaited ribbon. Finally, the tables were threaded along their entire length with garlands of ivy and sprigs of white orange blossom, a truly mesmerising sight. Ian came across to her, he could see that she was overwhelmed.

"It's beautiful, isn't it? We've used most of the flowers from the garden, which was what Lucy wanted. It's been touch and go whether we'd manage, but friends from down the road came to our aid and filled their greenhouse with various pots to make sure we'd got enough for today."

"Magnificent, such a simple design but so effective," she turned to Ian and put a hand lightly on his arm. "I'm glad my outfit won't clash! Before I go, please show me where Grumps and I are sitting, he'll be so busy talking, he'll forget to look."

Ian took her to the table plan and then to the table itself, she made a mental note and then left Ian and her husband to get on with the final touches; there was no need for her to remain it was all so beautiful: now she must find Lucy and take care of her. So the morning passed with military precision and suddenly they were all sitting down to lunch, and except for the odd 'please' or 'thank you' or 'would you pass…' the table was silent. Lunch finished Lucy wanted to clear the table but was hurriedly 'shooed away to her bedroom for a quiet sit with her grandmother. Helen was delighted and set about arranging Lucy's room for ease of dressing.

"Please Gran, don't do that, just come and sit with me, I'm suddenly scared."

Helen looked at her granddaughter's pretty face now screwed up with worry and felt huge pity for the girl, she remembered her first wedding and how she'd felt, but then there'd been no one to talk to. Now she willingly sat beside Lucy and helped calm her nerves.

"Of course you are, it's only natural you should feel this way. You love Nick so much and don't want to fail him; now stop worrying yourself like this, it's normal to be scared, after all have you thought how he's feeling? He's got the responsibility of looking after you. Marriage is a huge commitment and the adventure ahead is one you're both going to get on with, through the bad times and the good. My advice to you is what's on my fridge door 'grow old with me, the best is yet to come'. And the best does come, but for now you've got to learn to live together, have rows together and love together; you're human and life's tough, but if you really love each other, then you can't possibly go wrong."

Lucy flung her arms around her grandmother, "I know you're right but I'm still scared and feel so inadequate."

Helen released her arms and looked hard at Lucy. "You do love him, don't you? This isn't just a fairy tale fancy is it? If it is, you must call it off now, no one will be angry; after all life's not a dress rehearsal it's for real and divorce is terrible, I know, I've been through it."

Lucy returned her grandmother's gaze clearly, "He's my life, Grannie, and I love him dearly, always will."

"Then there's nothing to worry about. Now, let's look in your handbag and see if your passport's in there and your money, make-up and phone. You'll have very little time when you come up to change, so let's make sure everything's to hand."

For the next ten minutes Lucy and Helen checked and rechecked everything; suddenly, the door burst open and there were her bridesmaids, "Are you ready for the off? Let's get you dressed." Helen greeted them all and was kissed many times, finally she looked at Lucy, who was happily blowing her a kiss before chattering away to her girlfriends. She left the room for her own and the long process of dressing began.

When Helen returned to their room, she found her husband sleeping peacefully on the bed, his morning coat carefully hung up on the wardrobe door and his shoes cleaned and tidily placed beside the bed. She tip-toed around to her wardrobe and removed her suit from its covering and laid it on the bed, next she opened the hat box and took out her crowning glory, 'the Hat'. She'd told no one about her outfit only Lucy last night, she wanted to be a surprise for a change; she knew that her daughter would dislike anything she wore, so had chosen her outfit to suit herself. It was a plain lavender and green shot silk dress and jacket, the only exception being the buttons, which were a deep amethyst and emerald green colour – her jewel colours, she'd found them in a junk shop and she loved them. The hat was a simple straw with an upturned brim on one side, trimmed with a band and large bow in the same fabric as the outfit. Last night she pinned her amethyst and diamond brooch to the bow and now surveyed the effect, with satisfaction; 'Yes,' she thought, 'just my pearls and that will be enough!' Within a short while she was dressed and surveying herself in the long mirror and didn't hear or see the figure of her husband behind her.

"Yes, my dear, you look very elegant as always, and I like the colour, suits you well."

She turned and gave him a big smile, "I'm so glad you like it, I really want to look good for Lucy and of course, for you, and I don't want to look 'overdone'."

"You certainly don't look like that." He watched as his wife picked up her bag and gloves and slipped into her shoes; he opened the door and together they went down to the rest of the family, who were in the drawing-room waiting for the cars and to see the bride. Suddenly, Lucy appeared, to Helen's eyes a vision of amazing serenity and beauty; the rest of the family were speechless for a moment and then the comments started and the first of the tears flowed. Sophie appeared quietly and proudly behind her daughter, and for once, looked fabulous, she wore a long deep crimson dress to her ankles with matching shoes and a small tricorne hat in the same colour perched on her dark hair. She looked up and caught her mother's eye, Helen blew her a kiss of approval and love. Helen felt a tug on her sleeve it was Lucy, a delicious confection of old lace, perfume and happiness, her eyes sparkled as she held up her right hand.

"Look Granny, my something 'old', I had to wear it now as well as later when I go away, I love it so much." She tried to kiss her grandmother but couldn't, too much veil and silk between them, so they kissed the air instead and laughed.

"You look radiant, my dear; just as you should, be very happy always."

"Come along, Mother, Grumps is in the car and it's time for you to go, we can't hold up the proceedings for too long." Helen turned and looked at her daughter, who was smiling and so proud. "By the way, I like the outfit very much, you look great."

Helen was so surprised at her daughter's comment that she almost forgot to thank her, but thank her she did by gripping her hand and giving her a quick peck on her cheek.

"Thank you dear, I really appreciate that and now I'll see you in a little while in church, don't forget the dogs." She went down the steps to the car and climbed in beside Grumps and waved back at the happy faces, and they were gone. Soon they were at the church and walking up the aisle to their seats. The air was heavy with the scent of flowers and the mixed perfumes all around them, so many young people and so many old friends, who greeted them both cheerily. Helen slipped into the pew behind Sophie and Ian's, and she and Grumps were greeted fondly by their friends; Vicky was resplendent in vivid blue and her usual signature rubies, Tessa was in cream and Stella in deep green, the men equally resplendent in morning coats and cream silk waistcoats. The friends resumed their places and waited for the main party to arrive, and they didn't have to wait long. Suddenly, Sophie appeared beside Helen and Grumps.

"Why, whatever's the matter?" said Grumps, quickly standing up.

"Nothing serious really, it's just Lucy. Mum, have you a spare hanky, Lucy's just had a bout of tears and used mine and now is frantically doing her mascara again; it never rains but it pours, thank goodness I've only one daughter, I couldn't do this again."

Helen handed her a handkerchief. "Don't worry dear, it's only nerves, at least she's not feeling sick."

"Oh heavens, don't say that, that really would be tempting fate!" As swiftly as she'd appeared she disappeared, only to reappear five minutes later, walking sedately to her place in front of her mother. She turned around and gave a 'thumbs up' sign; it was then that both Helen and Vicky realised that it wasn't Lucy who'd cried but Sophie.

"Well, that's one way of trying to cover up a 'Sophie moment', isn't it?" said Vicky, giving Helen a knowing wink.

"Shush, she'll hear, but at least I wasn't in the car with her at the time."

"What a relief!"

The two friends giggled at each other just as a fanfare from the organ started and they all stood for the entrance of the bride on her father's arm. Ian's face was a picture of proud happiness, and he couldn't stop looking at his beautiful daughter as with fatherly reluctance he delivered her to Nick's side, and so the ceremony began. The vicar was an old friend and had known Ian and Sophie for many years and baptized their children and watched them grow. He'd come to the village at roughly the same time as Sophie and Ian and apart from a long stint in India and Zimbabwe, he'd never really left the parish but devoted himself completely to the community. The bishop wanted him to move to the cathedral but he'd resisted any form of promotion, preferring to be in a place he knew and loved. Soon the age-old words rang out, "Who giveth this woman to be married to this man?" and Ian's response equally strong, "I do." His job done, he returned to his wife and took her hand.

Grumps read the lesson and Helen watched him and thought of all the different places they'd been to and how their lives had prospered over the years. They'd had some very tough times, illnesses and almost bankruptcy but through it all his sense of humour and terrier-like tenacity to win had won through every time. He returned to his seat and the service continued, with the vows being taken and the rings exchanged (Grumps did not approve of rings on a man's finger, 'He'll lose it within a month' he'd said) however, he watched as they were exchanged and muttered under his breath. The service ended, two enormously happy people walked down the aisle, closely followed by the rest of the bridal party out into the sunshine that greeted them. The little church emptied quickly and soon the air was full of happy conversation and the inevitable photographs. Helen was aware that her grandson was standing beside her very quietly, not joining in nor smiling.

"What's the matter, Paul? You look so sad, this is your sister's wedding day you should be happy for her and your new 'brother-in-law', you've now another family."

"I know Gran, and I am happy for Lucy I really am, but...well...let's just say I'm wrapped up in my own thoughts, I'll be all right soon especially when I can have a drink."

He turned and smiled at her and sauntered away and was soon in deep conversation with a very handsome stranger. Helen had a sudden déjà vu and the past loomed large and filled her with foreboding, 'Not again, surely not again,' she thought to herself. Grumps' arm was around her waist, turning her away from the scene and her thoughts.

"Come along, old girl, time for the off and dinner, I'm beginning to fade, and Neal and Peter agree with me that we need a drink, and I know very well that you girls will be parched too with all your chattering."

He steered her back to their friends and soon they were all safely in the car, cramped admittedly, but all together. When they arrived back at the house, all was fun and noisy chatter, glasses clinked and hugs and kisses were freely exchanged. Helen and Vicky went upstairs to the bedroom, and Helen happily kicked off her shoes and got rid of the 'Hat' and her gloves. They adjusted their make-up and Helen paused and looked out of the window at the people milling below. Vicky came and stood beside her

"What's up, dear? You look as if you've seen a ghost."

"I think I've seen one from the past, and I'm not sure what to do...an ugly spectre, and now I think it's connected to my grandson, Paul."

"You mean his gay friend, don't you?" Helen looked at Vicky in disbelief and tried to speak, "It's all right, we've all guessed, including Grumps. It's hard, I know, but try and accept it and enjoy the rest of today. Paul will want you to meet him, try and do so...amiably; at least this time, you don't have to experience anything, that job falls to Sophie and Ian. Sophie will be very conscious of your feelings and will need to talk at a future date, just bear that in mind."

"I don't know what to say, I'm very numb all of a sudden and my instincts are to save Paul from the pitfalls of this relationship. God, how I hate gays and buggery, it's all so unnatural! Oh heavens, what have I said, that's so wrong; I don't hate them just what *it* stands for." Vicky gave Helen a glass of water, she took a sip and pent up beliefs and frustrations came to the fore. "I tell you there'll be no procreation as we know it ever again, everything will be born to order and choice. Society will break down, it's just as Grumps said, 'decline and fall', no morality or common decency anymore."

"Helen, come on don't think like that, what happened to you in the past is over and done with, try and think of this as a true and loving partnership that's been forged on the same principles as you and Grumps or Sophie and Ian, something built to last."

"Yes, I'm sorry, but it'll take a hell of a long time to understand it if ever. I've such a deep seated hurt inside me and remember, it all happened before and during Charlotte's cancer and death, so the ugliness is permanently there, wound up with an innocent child."

Vicky paused, "I know it's hard," she patted her friend's hand, "but I'm always here to help and listen, just like Bill and Pauline did all those years ago; what a shame they're not here. Come on, let's go down."

Vicky took Helen's hand in hers whilst Helen put on her shoes again and together they went downstairs and re-joined the party. It had been a lovely day and still was, the sun was beginning to set in the valley and bathe the garden in a golden light as they went in for dinner, the night jars started their evening hymn and a robin and blackbird chirped away with them in descant, bees buzzed in the roses and the midges started dancing in the sunbeams; peaceful happiness and tranquillity settled like a mantle across the bucolic sight. The evening progressed and once dinner was over and the speeches made, the dancing began. Grumps took the girls in turn onto the floor and even had a 'quick one' with Lucy. Finally, he came and took Helen in his arms and they took to the floor, quietly he guided her across the room to where Paul and his friend were sitting, he bent down and whispered in her ear, "I know you've guessed just as we all have, now go and put the boy out of his misery and meet his pal; it's not what we're used to, I know, but put Paul's mind at rest; you mean rather a lot to him and he knows he's hurt you by probably reviving old memories. Just remember, tomorrow we go home to our home, well away from here and to our friends and our normality."

He released Helen and turned to Paul and Francois, "Here she is, Paul, come to speak to you and Francois." She looked at Paul and the handsome stranger beside him.

"Grandma, this is Francois. He and I live together in London but our work takes us to Paris as well and that's where we met. Francois, this is my grandmother, Helen."

Helen extended her hand, "How do you do, Francois? I'm happy to meet you, I'm afraid my French is not good, otherwise I'd greet you in your mother tongue."

Francois, with true Gallic gallantry, lifted Helen's hand to his lips and bowed over it, "I, too, am glad to meet you and I hope that you'll come to Paris sometime and I can show you the sights and give you dinner." Two twinkling brown eyes met hers and instinctively, she relaxed and smiled.

"I look forward to that with pleasure, I've not been to Paris for years."

Francois linked her hand through his arm. "Then you must come soon, I understand you love art – so do I – we will see the galleries together."

"I'd like that very much." She turned and kissed Paul and squeezed his arm, "I'm so glad I've met your friend Francois, what a delight he is, I hope you both remain happy together for many years."

Grumps said a cordial goodnight to them both and took Helen back onto the floor and held her close, she was shaking very badly and felt nauseous. "Well done, I know that was hard for you, but you've put Paul at ease, thank you for that." Helen stared at her husband, not comprehending his attitude, he went on, "It's not what we believe in but for the moment we must acknowledge that Paul and Francois are happy. Now I must confess something to you and as this is probably the most romantic spot in the whole room, I'll go ahead, I love you so much and can never imagine a day without you. How I wish we'd met years ago and how I would have loved you then."

"Oh Grumps, my darling Grumps, I love you so much too, but if we'd married all those years ago, by now we'd have been at daggers drawn." They laughed and he held her closer. "Let's just enjoy the years we've had and the ones to come, but remember and never forget that you mean the world to me and always will."

He took her back to their table. Vicky said, "I'm leaving soon, and Tessa and Peter are going to take me home in the morning." During the ensuing babble they all decided that this party was never going to end until the small hours, so the decision was made to leave early and say their farewells and thanks. Finally, Neal suggested that they all meet at the pub at home for a late lunch to round off the weekend, this was greeted with cries in the affirmative. Grumps said that they'd be late, he and Helen not being able to leave until mid-morning, so could they meet at four, and so it was decided.

A cry from the back of the room declared that the "bride and groom are leaving" and they all raced as one to the front door to wave them off. The car was suitably decorated with old shoes, pans, horse shoes and a liberal spraying of 'just married' over the bonnet and boot of the car, and suddenly they were gone with Lucy leaning across the boot and waving like mad to the assembled company.

"Well, that's all over, what a day! Now let's all have a final drink to 'one for the road'," said Grumps, they all looked at him in amazement. "Well, it's been a great wedding and we've all survived."

'Collapse of stout party,' thought Helen and thought longingly of her bed, which for the moment was to be denied; she watched as her husband retrieved another bottle of champagne and he, Neil and Peter tried to devise a way of opening it so as not to damage their suits, as usual Tessa and Stella did it. Soon the seven friends were happily drinking a final night-cap and to the day just ending. They'd meet again tomorrow, the events of today being recounted in happy and contented detail in the tried and tested familiar surroundings of their local pub.